## Miki & Garrett Ward

We dedicate this book to our
family. To Shawna and Patti
who change the atmosphere
around them like unicorns.
-Miki and Garrett

# FLESH & BOLD

## MIKI WARD
## GARRETT WARD

MIKI AND MINE LLC

Cover Design by Christina Schneider at MikiandMine LLC
Editing by Robin Lee Rainy Day Editing
Formatted by Zoe Parker
Copyright © 2018 Miki Ward & Garrett V Ward
Published by Miki & Mine LLC

# CONTENTS

# NOTE FROM THE AUTHORS

# Flesh & Bold

Miki & Garrett Ward

# SAME OLE SAME OLE

*T*he icy wind is tearing at me as I walk to the library where I work. *You can do this, just put one foot in front of the other.* I've been crying for three days now because of my loser of a boyfriend. I'm done with that. I won't give him another thought. In fact, I'm not ever repeating his name. Best to forget that Freddie Ray ever existed. Just get on with my life and have fun for a change. Then, I can do what I want and not what someone else tells me to do.

*You go girl.* I smile to myself as I open the heavy doors and slide a little on the ice as the weight of the door pulls me. I catch my footing, and I'm able to put some force into it. As I start to pull it open, a strong arm reaches over me and easily pulls the door open. The wind blows a spicy scent to me, and I take a deep breath enjoying the thought that this guy might pay attention to me. Nope, definitely not. Instead, he holds the door with an irritated look waiting for me to go through. I hurry in, and he rushes off. Okay, whatever buddy. There has to be a good takeaway from that action somewhere. Yep! He opened the door, and I'll take it.

I head over to the front desk and check in on the computer, then walk over to a door a few feet away leading to our coat room. The few of us who are employed here at the city library each have a bin in a large cupboard. I put my coat on a hook on the wall and lock my purse in my basket then return to the front desk and take my place. It's not much, but I get a paycheck that pays the rent and provides all the reading I want. Plus, as a bonus, I don't get in trouble for reading at work or playing on my computer.

The early part of my shift is when I first check my email. It's usually quiet at shift change because of the overlapping employee coverage. For some reason, the city likes to keep the outgoing staff for an hour while the incoming team is getting ready for their shift. Anyway, my first message is one that I've been getting for the past several months. My mouse pointer is sitting above the trash icon... *What the heck... just re-read it.* This email is different than the average job offer. It doesn't have a company letterhead. It's written more like a note from a friend. It says;

---

Dear Miss Rollins,

I have a very unique opportunity for you if you choose to accept our job offer. I believe you are just the person who can fill this position. We are looking for someone who can adjust to a changing environment and deliver sterling results. The job comes with several perks, your own home in a beautiful area out of the city, health benefits, paid vacations, and a personal assistant. If you wish to interview for this position, please reply to this email with your rsvp then meet me Saturday at the Carlon

hotel downtown, and I will treat you to a dinner at
7:00 pm.

Sincerely yours,

Mae Thorough - HR

---

OK, THIS ISN'T THE SAME ONE THAT I'VE IGNORED BEFORE. BUT
what in the ever-loving kinkajou is this? It has to be SPAM.
I'm kinda interested. I'd love a change. Can this offer be real?
I better talk to Anthony, my best friend from forever, and see
what he thinks. I mean really, dinner at the Carlon would be
great, and if nothing else, I would get a great meal. It's worth
considering, and I have four days to mull it over.

The jerk who opened the door throws a large book up on
the counter and says, "I need to check this out."

"Certainly, do you have a library card which you can scan,
or shall I open you a new account?" I ask. He needs a new
account, so I make small talk with him as I create the
account. He leaves, and my day progresses the way most of
my work days do––full of nothing special.

When I lock up, it's dark, and the cold is even more biting
as I walk to my car. Anthony installed an app on my phone
which has an emergency button that I hold until I get in my
car and lock the doors. He says it'll call 911 and message him
if I take my finger off the button for more than ten seconds
without disabling the app. It makes me feel better when I'm
alone in the dark. I pass a few people on my way through the
parking lot, but they're too busy to notice me or even nod. I
should make it a point to say hi to at least one stranger every
day. Starting tomorrow, I'll do that, whether they say hi back
to me, or not.

My dad told me when he was alive that I should smile at others, and that a gesture of positivity would bring good back to me. He didn't have any idea what the world is really like. I was a high-risk pregnancy for my mother, and she passed in childbirth. My dad was already in his late fifties when I was born, he passed while I was in college a few years ago. He was my best buddy besides Anthony.

I grew up with that screwball best friend of mine. Anthony and I were born within a few months of each other, and he lived in the house next to mine. We were always together and still are. We promised when we were in the first grade that we would marry when we grew up. That was before he figured out he likes men way more than women. He says I'm still the only girl for him, just not in a sexy way, even though he tells me I'm beautiful.

I stop at the convenience store in my neighborhood and get us each a deli sandwich and some coffee then head the rest of the way home. Ice crunches under my tires as I pull into the driveway. I see Anthony is already home. He's been rooming with me since my father passed. It started out to take care of me until I got my feet under me. His parents wanted to travel, the next thing we knew, they are selling their house and buying a travel home. They're thrilled to be traveling, and Anthony and I are glad to be roomies. I keep the house clean, and he makes it beautiful.

I grab my bags and open the car door. I carefully set my feet on the ice-covered driveway. *I don't want to fall.* As I walk to the door, I take little steps to be careful. Before I take out my keys, Anthony opens the door and gives me one of his brilliant smiles. He takes all my bags and holds my hand to help me into the house. I take my shoes off and kick them under a bench in the foyer. Then I hang up my coat and toss my hat and gloves on the foyer table. He sets our sandwiches on the counter and my purse on the front table with my gloves so I can remember where they are. I can never keep up with where I left my purse if Anthony doesn't put it in the same spot for me.

I give him a big hug, and he says, "Roja," he's been calling me that since we were little because of my red hair. I let him. "I had the best day today. I met this guy with the cutest cleft chin, and I have a date this weekend. I'm so excited. How was work?"

Taking a breath, I pause for a sec then I say, "My day was fine, just like normal. I'm happy for you. When do I get to meet Mr. cute chin?"

"Soon, just let me see if it's going anywhere first. I hate to make him feel like he's meeting my family before we've even gotten to know each other. I'm sorry you had no exciting action today. We've got to find something to spice up your life." He fishes out a small pot and dumps a can of soup stock in it and starts pouring in some vegetables. "This'll be ready in a few. Would you like to watch a movie while we eat?"

"Sounds fun. Do I get to pick tonight?"

He nods me a, "yes" while stirring the soup. I start looking up a movie. I'm in the mood for an adventure flick. If I can't have a real one, at least I can watch one and pretend I'm part of it while I watch.

He plates our food and brings it to me on the couch as I hit the play button for the movie. We set our bowls on the coffee table when we finish eating. The film is such a dud we stop it and decide to talk instead. I fill him in about the email, and he wants to see it, so I get my laptop, and we squeeze together so we can both read it. He pops me on the knee and says, "You should check it out, Ro. I'm not even kidding. Put my number on speed dial, and I'll be there as fast as I can get there if you need me. In fact, I can take my date there, and I can give you moral support."

"No, I don't want you to ruin your date for this. You really think I should go?"

"Yes, at least for dinner. You need a change to get over that slob you've been letting control you. I say be brave, do this for yourself. At least see what she has to say--and order the cheesecake." He hits reply, and I type in my RSVP. He hits send making me smile. It feels good.

"Haha, you boob. I love you," I declare as I get up and take the dishes to the kitchen. I load the dishwasher, say good-night to Anthony, and go to bed. I sleep and dream about a man who I feel like I know but haven't met in reality. I've dreamed of him many times before and would love to know him. He's a ginger but different from me. His hair is amazing. Its lighter than my bright copper locks he's almost blonde and, up to date, with a long on top short on the sides cut. He's a lot taller than my five feet six inches, so he's got to be over six feet. His muscles alone would make me look twice, but his face is the draw. Oh... I'm just going to appreciate this man for a while as I drift deeper into sleep.

## MEETING MAE

*T*oday is the day I'm finally going to meet Ms. Mae Thorough at the Carlon. Anthony and his date will already be there before I arrive. Right now, I need to get ready. I have a pretty black lace dress I want to wear with my knee-high black boots––but what else?

I call out, "Anthony are you still here? I can't decide what to wear with my lace dress and boots."

He comes in and goes straight for my closet and pulls out some thick black tights and a designer scarf then he hangs my teal duster on the outside of the door. Wear your gold jewelry, and it'll pop. Not too much just earrings, a necklace, and maybe a couple of bangles.

"Thank you," I say and kiss his cheek.

"I'm leaving now and will see you there. I have to get a haircut. You got this red-hot Roja." He blows me a kiss and leaves.

I manage to cut myself on the ankle while I was shaving. Good thing I'll be wearing boots and no one'll see. I must be nervous. "Shawna Ro Rollins," I don't have a middle name, but Anthony and I added the Ro years ago, and I'm used to saying it, "you are a force, a bold woman who wants this. Be brave." I try to clear the negative thoughts from my mind then finish getting ready.

When I finally lock the door and start for the car, I'm smiling. I want this. Driving to the Carlon went by in a blur, the whole trip was unnoticeable, just like my life. I'm changing that tonight--I hope.

The doorman holds the door for me and tips his hat. I love that. I'm taking off my gloves when the receptionist glances up waiting for me to respond to her unspoken request for my name. I introduce myself, and with a smile, she says, "Right this way, Miss Rollins. If you will please follow me."

I nod to her and follow, impressed. The room is extravagant and richly decorated. She takes me to a small table in an alcove away from the mainstream of customers. I do see Anthony, he pats my leg as I pass his table. His date is very good looking. I'm happy about that for him. Hopefully, the guy is as wonderful as he looks.

Sitting at the table, apparently waiting on me, is a woman who appears to be in her early forties. Her hair is entirely silver though, and her eyes gleam with a fantastic spark. She's a woman who knows who she is, and it isn't a pauper. She waves a hand and nods at the waiter who was already walking toward my chair. He smiles at her wave and greets me with, "Welcome to the Carlon, Ms. Rollins," as he neatly pulls out my chair to seat me. Mae Thorough stretches out a hand to shake mine. She has a gentle touch and soft skin.

"I'm Mae darling. I have to say I'd heard that you look like your mother, but the similarities are stunning, just like you. Would you like a drink?"

My heart stops. Father did share that with me, but I've

never met anyone else who knew my mother. I'm quite shocked. "Ma'am, did you know my mother?" I ask.

"Yes, darling, I knew your sweet mother. Delaney was in my classes when we attended school. In fact, she was my best friend. I have something which I will give you that belonged to her if you take the position I'm offering. It was a gift from her to me when she left... our hometown to start a new life with the love of her life."

"You don't look old enough to have known her. Will you tell me more?" I feel the pull of this woman like a magnet. There is no way that I won't take the job now. I want to get to know her and maybe my mother through her.

She laughs, it sounds like a beautiful bell, then says, "Darling, I'm much older than I appear. Let's order and eat. We can talk business when we finish."

I order the prime rib. It turns out it's the most tender cut of beef I can ever remember having. I glance up and notice that Anthony and his date are ready to leave. I smile at him, and with a slight nod, I let him know I'm fine and will tell him about it later. He laughs as he and his handsome date leave. I order the cheesecake and coffee for dessert.

Mae and I talk like we've known each other for ages, and then she brings out a file folder and hands it to me. She says, "Shawna, this is a very generous deal, but if you find any part, not to your liking, we'll address that area to find common ground. I very much want you to accept this job. However, young lady, for you to make an informed decision, I must provide you with certain details which you may believe are fictitious. I assure you they are not. Shall I continue?"

"Yes ma'am, but I'm not sure I completely understand."

"Please dear, call me Mae. There will be a lot of information for you to absorb. I have learned that sometimes it's easier if you have some time to review the information before you're shown proof. Which I'm ready to show you just as soon as you deem this is something you wish to take on. Read the file dear. When you're sure you want to accept the position call me at the number on the card on the inside of the file. It's imperative you do not share this information, or I'll be forced to state this is simply a work of fiction from a movie we're developing. The people from this realm will take that as gospel just to ignore the truth. Do you understand?"

"Yes Mae, for now, but I do want you to know that I'm very interested and believe this is the change I've been waiting for. I'm hoping that you won't find another applicant and give them the position while I'm reading your file."

"I understand Shawna, be assured you are the only applicant who is worth my time. I will not be interviewing anyone else until I'm sure that you have refused me with a great deal of prejudice. Now would you like to order your friend some cheesecake to take home?"

"I smile at her concluding that we weren't as sneaky as we had thought. I answer, "Yes Mae, I would like that very much."

I tuck the file into my bag, then make my way home, feeling very happy and wondering what could be in the file. I want to dive right into it and find out all of the details, but I'm too exhausted to process that amount of information tonight with a clear head. I'll have to read it at work tomorrow, even though Sunday is usually a busy day at the library.

It's very late when I get to the house. In fact, Anthony is already asleep, so I put his cheesecake in the fridge with a note on it that says, "Take small bites and enjoy!"

# FACT OR FICTION

*I* arrive and check in at work. I'm excited to start examining the file that Mae gave me, so I don't bother to hang up my coat or lock up my purse. I go straight to my workstation, set my bag beside my chair and... wait. I have to wait to ensure I can read the file uninterrupted and remove the possibility of wandering eyes reading over my shoulder.

Sundays are somewhat busy here as many of the students choose today to make the final adjustments to their school-work for the coming week. I guess if I'm being honest just as many kids are starting their homework today as those who are finishing it.

In any case, it takes me until lunch to get caught up and for visitors to settle down to their computer stations. Feeling at ease and that no prying eyes will take a peek at my... ummm reading materials. I sit at my desk and finally pull out the file to start reading. The record reads like a fantastical fictional story, not a family history. It clearly states that my family is part of a dynasty of a particular hill country. I have no idea where this country is situated. But according to this file, I have a family residence located there. The name of this mysterious country is Elser.

Apparently, my mom was some kind of a revered leader there. There's paperwork in this file which says that my mother was given to my father in marriage to seal a debt to the Earth realm. This doesn't make any sense. I've seen old photos, and they are pretty clear my parents loved each other very much. My dad even told me they couldn't tolerate being apart. The documents also state the marriage will, '... make the passage here only a mark away.' I'm not sure what a 'mark' is. Could it be a measure of distance... like a mile? Not sure I understand any of this. I must be missing something important, so I make a note to ask Mae when I talk to her again.

Another thing, the story is signed by the Royal Wizard, Jatter the Hart. Maybe Mae accidentally gave me the wrong file. I plan to read the entire thing anyway, even if I have to stay up all night.

An alarm pops up on my computer, reminding me it's time to start closing up the library. I stuff the file back into my bag and press the button to play the canned closing message. A robotic voice clips, "The building will be closing in ten minutes. Please make your final selections or save your work, then make your way to the front exits." I play the message twice and check to ensure everyone is leaving. I also give a nod to Tyler, the security guard, so he can do his sweep and verify that everyone is gone.

After seeing that the last visitor has left, I head back to clean up the break room and the coffee pot. I'm already in my coat and putting on my gloves and hat when Tyler comes walking toward me escorting a man who is clearly down on his luck. This gentleman is probably planning on crashing here to avoid sleeping out in the frigid winter wind.

"Thank you, Tyler," I say and then ask the man, "Sir, do you have a place to stay tonight?" The man shakes his head. I tell him, "Come with me. I'll take you to the shelter and make sure you have a bed. Is that okay?"

He smiles and nods. I have a feeling that he's harmless. My gut feelings have not ever steered me wrong, so I'm not afraid. Tyler smiles, and we leave the building. After I've stopped at the shelter with the homeless man, I walk inside with him and talk to the receptionist. "Are the meals still being served?"

"Yes, ma'am they are." The young receptionist states.

"Good. I have a friend who needs something warm to eat and a bed to sleep in."

"You're in luck. We have both of those here. We also have conversation, legal aid, and even spiritual aid for those so inclined. The cafeteria is over that way." The young receptionist says as he points the direction to the cafeteria.

On the ride over, I learned the man I was driving to the shelter is named Tom. I ask him, "Would you like me to sit with you for a while?"

"No, ma'am. I'll be okay." Suddenly, out of thin air, he reaches to hug me. Ooo, when was the last time he had a bath? He smells like it wasn't anytime within the last decade! Almost as fast, I chastise myself for having such a pathetic thought. My father taught me to care most for those who have the least. Shame on you, Shawna Rollins. I reach for him and pull him in tightly hugging him until he lets me go. I may not be rich, but I can be rich in love, affect my world positively, and maybe influence others by my example.

I hold him by the shoulders and advise, "Tom you'll be

safe here. Come and visit me during the week at the library if you want to, and I'll give you a ride back here, okay?"

He has tears in his eyes and nods to me that he will. I make my way home in time to see Anthony just leaving. I'm happy––I have a great takeaway for today.

He rolls down his window as I get out of my car and says, "Hey red hot Ro, I left you some dinner in the microwave. I like the guy I was with last night, and we have another date. We're going skating tonight. I'll be late, so don't wait up. His name is Don Avery." He informs me with a grin.

I'm happy for Anthony. He's such a kind and caring person, and he deserves to be happy. I sigh and declare with a smile, "You have fun mister. Be safe, and tell me more when you can. I want details since I have to wait." I wink, and he drives away laughing.

A night alone is the norm for me even though I do have Anthony sometimes. That gets me wondering, what if it's time for Anthony to get serious and find a real relationship? Maybe it's time he gets on with his life and not have to take care of me any longer. I panic a little, it seems plausible… like I might be holding him back from a real life. The strange thing is, I'm not sad about him moving on because I want my bestie to have a fantastic life. For that to happen, I have to be okay with us not being together all the time anymore. Maybe I'm ready to have a real life of my own too. Like what idiot, like taking the job Mae offered. The thought excites me, and I start heating my dinner.

While the microwave hums I take the file out of my bag and set it on the table before getting some water to drink. The micro beeps and I sit down to eat and read. There is a picture of my parents in this file. I have this same picture in the living room above the mantel. No, I look closer, this picture is very different. I'm one hundred percent positive that this is my parents. Holy Cow! As I reexamine the image, I'm sure I see it correctly... my mother with a large set of white wings. She looks gorgeous and a little otherworldly. My dad looks so handsome and has his large hand on her waist. He looks just the way I remember him, just younger. I drop the picture and sit back in my chair in shock.

Unsure of what to do, I get up and start cleaning. When the whole kitchen is spick and span, I walk back into the living room. I get the picture of my parents off the wall and bring it to the table. While I was cleaning, I figure out that someone had to have photoshopped wings on my mom for some reason. As I study the picture that I've had hanging on my wall for so many years, I notice that part of the trees in the background are missing their middle! Quickly, I go to my room to grab a magnifying glass then race back to the kitchen table. In the place where the wings are in the picture from the file, the trees are covered by my mother's wings. That can only mean one thing... the picture that was photo-shopped must be... my picture. The one that I've seen all my life and never noticed anything out of the ordinary.

Freaking fairy tales! The rest of the file might be right too. In a near panic, I close it and refuse to read another word. I go straight to bed. Maybe, just maybe, I can fall asleep and dream about the handsome ginger again.

# MAKING THE CALL

*a*n eruption of a low metallic note rumbles through my room startling me awake. Instantly I jump out of bed to check out what the source could be. I grab my childhood tee ball bat from beside the door on my way to investigate. My first stop is to check on Anthony. I find him sprawled lengthwise across his bed uncovered. He's in his silky Pikachu boxers and still has his socks on. I take off his socks and cover him with a blanket from the rocker in the corner. Then I go to check the rest of the house. The microwave registers exactly 3:00 a.m. on its green digital display. The house is now silent. A silence which is acutely different from the deep melodic tone that had jarred me awake a few minutes ago. *Maybe I was dreaming the sound.* I lean my small bat against the wall, its home beside my door and lie down. After laying there pretending to try to fall asleep, I determine that I've scared myself enough, I take my bat and go back to Anthony's room to lay down with him.

I smell coffee and wake to a bright sunny morning. I begin the welcoming stretch of a comfortable sleep. Well, at least the last part of the night was pleasant. Is that coffee? Yes! And it's calling my name. I can hear the shower, so I get up to get us both a cup of coffee. Anthony comes out of the bathroom just as I finish pouring his cup. I hand it to him, and he asks, "What happened last night Shawna, did I miss a break-in?"

He's so cute. I smile and utter, "No I scared myself a bit, I went to bed and woke at three convinced that I heard a noise. Oddest thing, though. I thought it sounded like a horn. I'm guessing you farted."

We both laugh, and he says, "You might be right. I was holding one all night, so I wouldn't get embarrassed in front of Don. Our relationship is not to the "it's okay to fart in front of each other yet" stage." I'm nearly crying, and my face hurts from laughing.

"What had you scared?"

It's my day off and I don't have to get ready, but he has to be at work in an hour, and it's a thirty-minute drive. I'm going to hurry and show him the pictures and see what he suggests. "It's this picture that was in this file the HR lady I met at the Carlon gave me," I say as I hand him the picture.

His eyes get huge as he notices the wings. When I hand him the other one to compare, I can tell by the look on his face that he sees what I see. "That's so odd, Ro, I would say it's photoshopped, but it looks like yours is the fake. It's weird. Do you want me to call in? I can stay with you and help you figure this out?"

That's what I don't want. Anthony putting everything off to take care of me. I might have to help him cut the apron strings. I better say this and get it out before back out. "No, I've got it. I want you to know that I'm planning to accept this job offer, and I may not be here when you get home. I'll text you if that happens though. I have some stuff I want to tell you as soon as we have some time. Go get ready for work. I promise I'm all right."

He smiles at me and touches the tip of my nose with a finger then takes off to get ready and leave for work. I go get in the shower. I always concentrate better in the shower, and I need to make a game plan. When I get out, I feel fantastic. I know what I want and what I'm going to do to get there. I want to know more about my mom, and this will at least let me know how she grew up. I get ready for my day then take a notebook and set it on the table by my file. I intend to go into this as prepared as I possibly can.

I'm shifting into an open frame of mind, a total must. I'm struggling to believe some of this is real, especially the Jatter the Hart thing. *Here's something.* The deed to the property located in Elser has a letter attached stating that I need to talk to the family solicitors within a week's time to go over distribution. I write a to-do list and set an alarm on my phone. I've read the entire file, and I still don't know what is real or precisely what my job will be. If it's a fantasy type theme park, then I'm sure I'll need some help.

Well, I'm not putting it off any longer. I grab my cell and call Mae with all intentions of asking her to meet me for lunch. She isn't answering so I leave a short message. Then I get my jacket and go out to the storeroom to find a suitcase. I'm a planner and want to be ready just in case Ms. Thorough calls and wants me to go and accept the offer in person. I really hope she does. Maybe I should suggest... and my phone rings before I unlock the door to the storage. It's Mae, so I pull off my glove and swipe to answer.

Oddly, it's a recorded message saying. Sorry, I missed your call. Will you please meet me at the Second Street Bistro at 1:00 p.m. today. I look at my phone as it hangs up, questioning the call. It seems like a real call because it has her number on the screen. I spend the rest of the morning filling the old luggage I'd retrieved and cleaning my room. I dress carefully, and with one last look at my phone, I rush out the door hoping to get some answers my brain will actually accept.

## MEETING IN ELSER

*I* leave my car in the parking garage and make my way down the steps to the sidewalk below. The ice is evident on this part of the sidewalk. Some of the ice that has melted in the sun has made its way down to part of the walkway and has frozen again in the shade provided by the tall parking terminal.

I cross the street and head toward the bistro. As I step onto the sidewalk again, I don't notice the ice. As I step on it, my feet slide out from under me. Instinctively I reach out and catch the arm of the guy walking next to me. Oops!

"Sorry about that," I relate as I chance an embarrassed look into his eyes. *What in the world? I just grabbed onto a faceless grim reaper. This guy is no kidding creepy!* With his hoodie low, I can't see his eyes; I swear I see glowing orbs where his eyes should be. I rush away and try not to look panicked. I hurry over to Mae who's sitting on a bench near the restaurant door.

I give her a quick handshake and smile as we go inside. I let her enter before me, and sneak a look behind me to check if Mr. Death Incarnate is watching. He's gone, or at least I can't see him, and I sigh a breath of relief.

Mae announces to the waiter there are two of us, and he seats us without a wait. I order hot chai tea and look over the menu, even though I know I'm getting a chicken club with potato salad on the side. I need a second to figure out how I'm going to say what I need to say. She takes the choice from me when she says, "Shawna I have a lot to relate, and not much time. I have to have you in Elser within one hour. The king is planning a small reception and requested our prompt attendance as he has other business."

Okay, that's surprising. A king, I should've known no decent fantasy is going to leave out the king. I shake my head a little at myself--this is crazy. Whatever... I'm going with it. "Well, we wouldn't want to disappoint the king."

Our waiter sets a cup in front of me with a tea-ball strainer which smells heavenly. He then pours hot steamy water over it and places a huge shortbread cookie on my saucer. I notice Mae has ordered the same thing and she's already removing her tea-ball and setting it beside her cookie. I like my tea strong, so I bob my strainer up and down a bit. I'm also trying to buy myself a little time, maybe I bounce it more than I usually would. When my drink is nice and dark, I take out the tea ball and set it on my saucer.

I start, "Mae I'm not going to beat around the bush. I'll be honest; I believe this is a fantasy story you have given me. The file reads like fiction, and yet the photo of my parents seems real. I have a similar photo, and it appears to have been doctored to remove wings which seem to be an integral part of my mother. They look suspiciously real. I'm entering a phase of my life where I feel I want change. I want adventure. Mae, I want to accept this position. Is it agreeable with you if I see the work site so I may be more informed?" I stop and bite my tongue hoping that I didn't sound like I had rambled through too much.

"Of course, darling, I need to escort you to the reception. Remember? The reception is your worksite, well at least part of it. The entire kingdom is your worksite," she answers.

Now I hope I don't have my, 'I have no idea what you're saying' face on when I answer, "Okay then it looks like we are going to a reception. Am I dressed appropriately, or should I change into something more formal?" I ask. As I complete my sentence, I see what seems to be a sly smile draw itself across Mae's face.

Mae easily transforms her smile into a loving version answering, "You're just fine Shawna, always beautiful. You seem to be taking this series of events quite well, so I'm going to be frank. At any time, if it's too much, just stop me." I nod my assent. "You will change when you get to Elser." Here she pauses just a heartbeat and catches my eyes. "It's not in this realm, at least as you would understand it. Elser is in an alternate realm much like the realm of the Tuatha De Danann in the fantasy novels here––only different. We do have a king. He's young and somewhat new at his job. But he's been groomed for the position since birth. His parents have passed on, just for your knowledge." Mae pauses as our waiter brings us a basket of hot bread and asks if we're ready to order. I could eat a horse by myself now. I'm a stress eater. So, I order a large pasta bowl and water. Mae gets soup and water.

Mae starts again by asking, "Are you okay? Have I gone too far?"

"I'm okay, and please continue, if you like?"

"Shawna, when I said you would change I didn't mean figuratively. I mean it sometimes is, but children who have parents who are from Elser have children who change to look like them upon entering the realm. Sometimes it's instant, and sometimes it's a process. So… I'm warning you, be prepared there could be physical changes as we step through."

There is a large table being seated near us, and many ears were too close for my comfort. I made small talk with Mae waiting for this group to settle down. I swear they were so noisy and move about so often that I wonder if they have lived in a big cave their whole lives. A pretty dark-haired woman with them finally quiets them, and I'm able to concentrate.

Just in time for our waiter to arrive with our food. We stay quiet while our waiter sets down our food. When the waiter is gone, I ask, "Like I might grow a pair of wings? You'll be with me though; you won't leave me, will you?" Maybe I should go over this again. I don't need a new life with adventure; I have books for that. I can stay in my boring lifestyle. Being alone for the rest of my life while my best friend moves on to the American dream couldn't be that terrible. Sadness starts to overwhelm me.

Mae must have been able to tell because she reaches across the table and holds onto my hand and says, "I won't leave you. I'll stay with you Shawna until you order me to leave."

We finish our lunch in silence. I feel awful, maybe I can't do this. "I need… have to go to the lady's room for a minute Mae please excuse me." Without waiting to hear her answer I take off. As I walk to the washroom, I pass a couple, obviously in love, hand in hand, and laughing. I feel better when I get to the bathroom and sit in a stall for a few minutes gathering my wits. I get up to leave and wash my hands and glance at myself in the mirror. My eyes are red, and that contrast makes the colors even brighter, I have one blue eye and one brown. I want what that couple outside has. If I remain introverted, chances are that I will not find someone––ever. I probably won't anyway, but at least I have a chance to be happy if I try something different. I feel so much better now that I've made the decision to tell Mae I'll go to Elser. With the decision made, I feel the sadness retreating; strength is returning. Okay, I'm sure, this is what will make me happy. It's scary, but no one ever conquers anything from their easy chairs, right? I walk straight back to Mae and blurt out, "I'm ready to go if you are."

She looks up and smiles with a quick exhale and takes my hand as we leave the bistro. We walk into a nearby department store. Without giving me time to back out, Mae enters a dressing room and motions for me to follow. I do with a raised brow. She plucks a marker out of her pocket and says, "Shawna, it's not a bad feeling, not at all, but it's fast, and it will pull you forward. Don't be frightened; it doesn't hurt. Hold my hand." I tighten my grip, and she writes a small rune on the wall and steps forward... into the wall.

It isn't solid anymore, and the wind rushes around me sucking me forward. It feels like when you can't help but walk fast when a high wind pushes you as you're walking on ice. A giddy feeling overtakes any nervousness. *I'm really doing this. Holy cow! It's real.* I do feel my body change! It doesn't hurt, but I have more than wings. I might not be exactly like my mother. I fancy that I blacked out for just a short moment before I realize Mae is speaking to me.

"Shawna, it's all right. We're here, and you did change, completely. Do you feel okay?"

"I do. I feel a little strange. I missed something. What do I look like, do I have wings? Uh oh." Even as I ask, I know that is not all that's changed. I look and have no hands, but I can see hooves on white legs. I'm starting to hyperventilate.

"Mae, am I a horse?" I ask looking around I'm in front of hundreds of people, and they are all clapping and hooting.

A man standing close to us comes over and gets down on a knee in front of me. Damn, he's fine. I hope I'm not drooling. He's even a ginger, just a lighter version than my copper locks. He has that long on top short on the sides cut that screams bad boy.

He says, "My most cherished lady, I'm Matt Dragonaire, King of Elser. We're so glad, Miss Rollins, to have you join us here in Elser. His voice is just as dreamy as the rest of him. The kingdom has long waited for the return of your kind. We need you. Nothing shall be withheld from you here. Whatever you need or want ask, and it'll be yours."

I'm not sure how long I stand there blinking like a total idiot. The crowd has gone silent waiting for me to answer, so I do my best.

"Thank you, Your Highness. Umm... Mae?" I squeak. I'm lucky I got that out. What I want to do is to run and hide.

"Darling, you are a unicorn. I'm both surprised, and yet, not at the same time. You're a dream come true," she says. The crowd is trying to get closer but are being held back by what looks like armed musketeers. I must be dreaming.

There's a man next to the king now, and he is saying that I have to change now so that the people will stop fawning and we must go to the castle. What? This man's wants are meaningless. I've got no clue how I changed in the first place! I didn't have much say so changing back is a hard no.

Mae steps closer and says, "Follow me, Shawna."

I do, and she takes me into a walled garden and closes a gate. *Now what?*

# MY FIRST CHANGE

*I* feel relief now that I'm no longer in front of that crowd. But now what? "Please Mae, what do I do? A unicorn? How? Why? What now?"

"Oh no no no, don't do that," she says.

"Don't do what? Panic! I dare you to be in my hooves and still be coherent."

"No darling, I didn't mean that. You're fading out, and I can just see your outlines to know where you are. I guess that happens to you when you feel scared or highly emotional; a defense mechanism likely. Can you calm down, take some deep breaths, and maybe think happy thoughts?" She asks.

I huff, "I'll try." I do take some deep breaths, and it sounds like loud blowing noises. I blink, irritated even more, then stop and remember dad and how he'd already been here. He knew about this place. He met mom here, and they fell in love. She loved him so much she left her home and came to the Earth realm giving up her life here. I remember dad was always so calm all the time. He would smile and...

"That's it darling. Thank the heavens you're visible again," Mae squeaks wringing her hands.

"Well that's good, and it was easy. What now?" I ask.

"Okay, now the way I usually change is by imagining the shift then the shape I want. Can you try that?" She pleads.

As I try, I feel a tingle and know my body is changing. It takes just seconds. I reach out, and my hand is in front of my face. Thank everything holy. My clothes shift with me, and I'm not standing here in my birthday suit like in the movies. I walk over to a cement bench and plop down, drained, trying to collect myself when the king bursts into the garden.

"What's taking so long? Why are you not out in the reception hall? Did you not notice your people are there to see and meet you?"

In my rush of emotion, his condescending tone sends me over the top. Hot ginger or not, I lash out. "Don't you have any manners? Or maybe you're incapable of considering anyone but yourself. Mae, can you take me home? I'm done, I don't believe this is going to work out for me."

The shocked looks on their faces doesn't affect me at all. I want to go home. *Unicorn! What the hell!* "Mae, I need to leave, now please," I repeat.

She looks down at me and nods. She takes out her marker again, and we walk to the nearby stone wall where she draws another rune. Like before I feel the wind pulling me though. This time, however, I'm at my own home.

"Thank you, Mae. I'll be in touch," I say quietly showing her to the door. She leaves with a dejected look on her face.

She turns to me and says, "Please reconsider, darling. We need you very much. The king is a dragon, hot-headed. He's young with lots of stress." Noticing the stone-cold set of my features she finishes, "If you change your mind you have my number. Please call me in a few days and tell me for sure what you decide." When I don't answer, she turns and walks out of my yard and down the street. I don't even ask if she needs a ride. I'm sure she has a rune for wherever she wants to go.

I walk into the house, and go to my room, throw off my clothes, then sink into bed and cry myself to sleep. My dream is so real, *I can taste salty air as I sit on a bluff by a rolling ocean. Gulls fly overhead, and a little pixie lands on a rock beside me. It's Mae and I let her hold onto one of my fingers. We sit and watch the water when my dream man puts a hand on my shoulder. I know it's him. It's my dream, so I sink into him feeling his strong arms surround me from behind. I fall deeper into sleep as we watch the waves together.* In the morning, I wake calmer.

Getting ready is a chore this morning. Anthony left a note for me on the creamer. He knows me so well. He says he has a business trip and will not be home for a few days. He'll text me from the airport. I feel so alone. I know I was simply overstimulated yesterday, and when king rump got in my face, I didn't react well. I guess if he's a hothead, like a dragon, I can be a flighty unicorn. Now to plan what I'm going to do and work this out in my head. I've got to go so I won't be late for work.

Half the day is gone, and I have done nothing but consider going back to Elser. Just how to do it and avoid the king... a delivery person from the florist walks into the library and comes to the front desk. She whispers, "This is for a Miss Rollins." I stammer that I'm her and she turns to leave. This vase is full of the most beautiful arrangement I've ever seen. Full of orange lilies. I take a deep breath sighing and open the note, it reads;

I will never forgive myself for being rough with you.
Please forgive a tormented stupid dragon. Matt

TEARS APPEAR AT THE CORNERS OF MY HAPPY EYES AND I SMILE.
"Okay," I whisper, "forgiven."

My heart is beating so fast overflowing with happiness
that I almost disregard the awful feeling I'm getting in the pit
of my stomach, but I don't. I quickly go into the break room
and stand so I can see out the door. Oh great! It's the faceless
guy in the hoodie who I grabbed the other day in the street.
The queasy feeling, I get is even worse than it was that day. I
wait, I'm hiding from him until he's gone. I can see smoke
coming from his breath and it smells like sulfur. He takes one
of my flowers and smells it then crushes it in his fist. That
dirtbag. He turns, departing rapidly. He slams the doors on
the way out. Thank goodness he's gone. My gut tells me this
is not just a stranger and my heart is telling me I want to go
back to Elser.

I take out my phone and text Mae notifying her that I'm
calmer now and can we have coffee when I get off work. She
answers immediately and says she'll be at the corner shop
waiting. I sigh feeling ready and know that I do want this
change.

When I reach the coffee shop, Mae is in the back, so I
order first waving to her. They have the best brownies, so I
get two for an apology. When I get my latte, I head over to
my new pixie friend and set a brownie in front of her and
say, "Mae I'm sorry. I was just over excited. I'm really an
introvert, just the thought of this type of adventure took me

to the edge. Then when the king snapped at me, I sort of lost it."

Her smile is heart melting. Then she answers me, "I understand darling. I'll be here if you want to talk about it."

"Which 'it' do you mean, the grumpy gorgeous king or my early departure?" I say smiling at her over my cup, and we both laugh.

"He is rather a grump, isn't he?"

"A handsome one."

We spend the next hour deciding that I'll try the trip again but with less fanfare and no king. We will meet at my family home in the forest she tells me. "You need to see the solicitor anyway." Like I know what a solicitor is in this fairy realm. I'm going with it, so I give her a date. I'll wrap up my affairs at work and make sure Anthony knows I'm going then in less than a week I can start a new chapter in my life.

Mae hands me a check and says it's the first installment of my moving bonus. After I'm in Elser for a month I'll receive the second installment, then a regular check, that is, if I approve.

"Ummm, there must be a mistake Mae. This is too much money," I say.

"No, it's just right for the job you're hired to do, Shawna. I assure you."

"Wow, this is wonderful," I gush.

The stranger might be of significance, so I alert Mae about him and what happened at work and she says with all seriousness, "I'm afraid we do have trolls who will hunt unicorns, and one who might be a dragon type. Can you fight at all, Shawna?"

My heart skips a beat, "I've had basic self-defense classes, nothing fancy. It's not in me to go down without a fight though." I have an idea she knows more than she can tell me right now.

"I don't imagine it's too serious since he was stalking you in public. Just keep yourself safe until I come to get you this weekend. I have to leave but before I do, do you need a bodyguard?" She asks.

"No, I'll be careful. See you this weekend." I get up as she leaves and hug her goodbye then gather my stuff and head home.

# REAL CHANGE

Finally, the weekend is here, and I'm itching to go. Anthony has already left since he's spending the day with Don. They're rock climbing, and both told me how happy they are for me and my new job. My bestie is going to stay at my house and take care of it for me. I didn't even worry when I gave my two weeks' notice at the library, and they let me quit early with no consequences. They would croak if they knew the details of my move. I told Anthony that I would call him later. I'll have to find out if that will work from Elser.

The knock on the front door doesn't surprise me as I set my last suitcase in front of it. That the king has come with Mae does surprise me. He reaches his hand out taking mine and says, "Shawna I'm so glad you are coming. Please forgive me for my actions last week. I'm a bloody tyrant at times."

"Of course, Your Highness, you're forgiven… if we can be friends." I coo. What the hell am I saying I can hardly make a coherent sentence around him.

"Oh, that's such a relief. I feared you would never forgive

me. Please let's be friends. You can call me Matt instead of whatever it was you thought when you left Elser. Ingrate or something. I'm sure it wasn't Highness," he laughs.

"Okay Matt, you can call me Shawna then," I say as Mae starts toward my pile of bags. Matt grabs up most, and I get what's left as Mae draws a rune on the wall and we all go through together. As we're swept into Elser, I drop my bags as I turn into a unicorn again. This time I have it figured out and change back just as fast. Looking around for my suitcase I see the most beautiful mansion in the middle of the forest. It seems as though it's almost part of the woods. With my mouth agape, I turn to Mae and Matt.

The king laughs at me and says, "Why yes friend, this is your home. The solicitors said they would be here when we arrive so let's enter, shall we?"

The mansion is made of large rocks that look like they had been pulled from the bottom of a river. The color of the stones tells me it's been here a very long time as I can see no stoneworking marks of any kind. We came in on the north-west side of the building so I can see two sides at the same time. The north side has the green patina of something like a Spanish Moss. The western side is covered with a green ivy which has been tended to form the shape of a tree on the front of the house. The home itself is nothing short of stunning. The home adds enchantment to the surrounding forest. The addition of the gardens completes the picture.

When we reach the steps leading up to the front door, a string of large buff men dressed in suits are waiting to help. The first introduces himself and the others, "Ma'am, I'm Howard, your house steward. This is your wait staff William, Turner, and David. I'll introduce you to the rest of the house-hold staff tonight if you desire." And if the king wasn't gorgeous enough, these guys are all in his same category of hotness. I'll never get a moments peace with them around. Mae walks in front of me and gently closes my mouth with two fingers to the bottom of my chin. She turns her silver head toward me and gives me a crooked little grin as she passes. I'll get her back. My eyes shift to Matt, yep he's watching me with a look of pure misery. Hmmm, maybe he... no couldn't be. I wink at him anyway. *Where did that come from you big flirt... all of a sudden.*

He races over and offers me his arm, and I take it. No way am I turning him down. I like him very much, and we're friends. His arm is hard muscle too. Yum.

I blink and stop dead in my tracks when we enter the foyer. This is really a mansion. I love it. It's my dream home with everything I could ever need, or want, I would bet.

Mae says, "Darling, I must be off. I leave you in capable hands. If you need me, you have my number." She gives me a quick hug. I turn to the king to see if he has goodbyes for her. He just nods, and when I turn back, Mae is already gone. Okay, I'll get used to that... maybe.

I lean just a little too far into Matt as I look at the room and he lets me. Yes, he's interested. I'm keeping him.

"It's amazing isn't it, friend? Your family has had it here for centuries and did well keeping it up for you to take over. Just in time." He motions us over to a doorway where a man is waiting. He introduces me, "Shawna Rollins, may I introduce you to your solicitor Mr. Villa and his team Mr. Canada and Mr. Kelly," the king says smoothly.

I reach out and shake their hands still wondering what 'just in time' means and say, "It's nice to meet you." Not knowing what else to say. This time, I make sure to close my mouth and let them begin.

"My friend, I'll leave you to your meeting... I guess. I

mean… well, you have a meeting." Matt says quietly looking at the floor.

"Please, Matt, will you stay with me? Do you have the time? I'll understand if you can't," I ask politely.

The look on his face and that he straightens his stance is a sure sign that he's glad I asked. He guides me into the room, and we sit down on one of the divans.

Mr. Villa begins by divulging that the estate passes to the closest living relative who is me as a granddaughter of the last owners. My mother was their older child, and I am the oldest grandchild.

"Mr. Villa I don't mean to be rude when I interrupt, but are there others in line for the estate?" I ask.

He nods seriously then says, "Yes ma'am, there is one other. You have a distant cousin on your maternal grandfather's side. He had an estranged brother who had a grandson who is the next in line after you. No other relatives are living in your family. I don't wish to upset you. Would you care for the details, Miss Rollins?"

"Yes sir, I do. Please continue," I say.

With a short nod, he begins his story." Your family is the only family of unicorns in the whole realm. They are known to help our people by bringing prosperity to us. The very air is cleaner when there is a unicorn in the forest. They are known to remove poison from toxic drinking water and streams, to be kingmakers, and unicorn blood can make a person younger. Unicorns can tell if a person is lying and compel the truth with a touch of their horn. Marriage to a unicorn can make their spouses live long lives unless the unicorn dies first then the bond dissolves so that the living partner doesn't die quicker from the loss. Madam, your grandparents were killed. They didn't die from old age. The constables are doing their best to find the killers, but they haven't had any luck. Your distant cousin was a suspect because he was here when the murders happened. However, he has an alibi from a, particularly believable party. The king's younger brother, Prince Barry, who was with him during a drunken spree. They are sure he didn't have anything to do with the killing or see anyone who could have committed the crime. I do apologize and hate to be the one to tell you. You have our condolences, Madam.

"Thank you," I utter not knowing anything else to say.

"Shall I continue?" He asks.

Taken aback with feelings for a family I didn't know, I look to Matt and nod slightly, he relays to Mr. Villa, "Please do." He takes my hand in his, calming my nerves and filling me with warmth.

He says, "The estate has a full staff, and they also reside on the property. You can change that as you desire. The land supports itself with thriving apple and peach orchards that provide fruit to the cities.

All bills including staff salaries and groceries are paid from our offices. You will have a monthly paycheck in the amount of 10,000 units. We do understand your monetary system and that amount equals to 100,000 American dollars. If you need an increase, I'll need to know in advance since this is not quickly completed in minutes. Here are your unit chips. They will be coded to you now if you will be so kind as to pick them up individually and wait until you hear the beep before moving to the other chip. One is for general spending one is for saving.

I do as he had instructed and watch the chip as it beeps and changes in my hand to say my name and shift form. It looks like a little unicorn now.

He starts again and hands me a large key which also beeps when I hold it. That was the key identifying you, Ms.

Rollins. It will only work for you and opens all the doors on the estate.

"I hate even to ask Mr. Villa, but do I have a car key or even a vehicle?" I ask.

"No ma'am, we can get you one if you want it after you encounter our mode of travel. Just be sure to contact me and let me know exactly what you would like, and I will attend to the matter. Here's a communication device which you might like. Again, if you want something else, please ask. He just handed me a necklace; I hope I have on my blank face, not my stupid face. If you would like to speak with anyone, press the latch on the chain and speak to who you wish to converse with including others in the Earth realm. If you would like to test it, we'll happily wait while you do."

"No… I've got it. I'll try later," I hedge.

"As you wish. The final step is for you to press your identity into the deed and the permissions paper which will permit us to pay your bills, and then our business today is concluded." I look at the document, and he touches a spot on the bottom indicating for me to touch it there. "Please hold your finger here for a couple of seconds." I do as he requests and authorizes both documents. The beep indicates when I should remove my finger from the paper. When we finish, he scoops everything up in a neat pile, puts it in his satchel and latches it.

I guess that it's my cue, so I ask, "Would you like some refreshments or something to drink. I'm sure I could find something in the kitchen." *I hope I have a kitchen.*

"No, ma'am. We have other business we must attend to."

I take their rejection with some level of happiness. So my friend, the king and I show them out.

With the business concluded and the solicitors gone, I take a deep breath and say, "Thank you, Matt. That was more stressful than I thought it would be. I need a bit of time to decompress. Do you mind showing me how to travel here? Maybe in the morning?" His surprised look has me backing up. "Oh, I'm so pushy, I apologize, I shouldn't have said that."

"No, my friend, I would love to do that with you. What time do you wake? I'll even take you for breakfast if you'll let me?"

"Can we sleep late and go at nine," I ask, smiling now.

"It's a date. Don't be late. I'm sure I won't be!" He says grinning back at me.

As I let him out, he touches my hand, the one that's holding onto the door frame. He keeps his hand over mine for an instant. When he removes his, he rakes his index finger down the side of my hand before he turns and leaves. I close the decorative door softly and lean against it with a sigh. Damn, he's so cute! I'm in crush with the man I thought I wanted to avoid forever.

# MY DATE

*I* stretch as I wake and look around the room. My whole-body smiles as I see the sunshine in the window. It's a beautiful day in Elser. I'm so happy. I know that I can get used to this awfully fast. How do I even tell what time it is here? There's a little red dot on my night-stand, so I press it, and a voice says, "May I help you, my lady?"

I say, "I need prepare to leave and need to know the time."

"It's eight thirty-two, ma'am."

Oh no! I jump out of bed and run toward my colossal bathroom. Halfway there, I turn around and race back to the red button and push it again. "Thank you," I say breathlessly. Turning, I again dash to the restroom.

I hear a distant, "Yes, my lady," as I jump in and take a flash shower.

I zoom around a hundred miles an hour with my hair on fire. Well, it's definitely a hair up day. I'm dressed and looking through my hair clips in no time. I choose one and tuck my rusty mop into it. I look pretty good, but I need some makeup. Dang... teeth. I brush my teeth in a way which would make my dentist grimace. Now makeup. I'm not the kind to do without, I like my war paint too much. But time... so 'five-minute face' it is. I hear a throat clear behind me and turn to see a tall woman with striped hair smiling at me.

I give her a crooked grin, and a raised brow then say, "The king is picking me up for breakfast... can you help?"

She bursts out laughing," I totally understand, my lady. Sit here, and I'll fix you right up." She takes the clip and brushes out my hair and re-clips it curling some of the stray wisps and pulling a few more free. It is beautiful now. We talk, and I find out her name is Jodi. She's a wolf shifter. She changes so I can see and changes back just as fast. I almost missed it and thought she looks a little more like a dog than a wolf. Well, what do I know? She's pretty either way, and I'm making her an ally. It seems she was here the whole time I was getting ready. We had a great laugh over that, but she agrees that if she were having breakfast with the king, she would be a wreck too.

"So Jodi, how do you tell time here anyway?"

"Well, usually by asking our talk. Here watch me." I watch her as she presses a chain at her neck then asks what time it is, and it answers in a sexy male voice. I look at her questioning with the secret girl look. She says we get to choose the voice we just need ask. I press my chain and ask the time and hear a childlike voice say it is 9:02 a.m. I love it. I'm going to keep this voice.

Then another voice from my doorway says, "My lady, the king is waiting on you downstairs. Do you wish to see him, or shall I send him away?"

I react quickly, "What? No, we have a date. I'm going to be gone today with him and not sure when we'll return. You're William, right?" *Really, I could turn the king away?*

He answers, "Yes ma'am, I am. I'll walk with you if you like." He nods to Jodi as he says this, and she tells me she'll be here when I return and to enjoy myself.

I'm not passing up walking with any handsome man. It's been too long for me, so I take his arm, and we head down to the king. I might be wrong, but I could swear William is smirking when we get to the king. He lets me go, bows, then leaves us.

Matt gives an almost imperceptible eye cut to William then ignores him and holds out an arm to me which I take. "Okay, my lady, are you ready to have some fun?"

"Most certainly, kind sir." We laugh, and he takes two markers from his pocket. Both are gold. He hands me one.

This one is for you, Shawna. We can practice after breakfast. Until then I'll drive if that's all right with you?" I nod. He takes his marker and makes a small rune on the door but before he finishes he shows it to me. It's a simple mark with straight lines. "Before I add the last line I use my shifter magic to envision where I want to go. It's that tingly feeling before you change. Ready?"

"Yes, let's go I could eat ah... not the right thing to say here... a whole lot." I improvise.

Matt laughs at me not fooled at all. He holds onto my waist and makes the last mark. As we're sucked through the gateway, I lean closer to him, and he tightens his grip some. We walk into a large restaurant, and the hostess reacts immediately asking where we would like to sit. She apparently is asking me and not the king, so I turn to him to include him, and he answers for me. "In the back please, we intend to take our time."

She seats us with deference, and our waiter is with us before she leaves. He introduces himself as John Pea and asks, "Madam, Your Highness would you care to hear our breakfast options?"

I answer for us both. "Yes please," I respond a little too excitedly.

The first option John Pea offers is pancakes. That's all I need to hear, and I interrupt him, "Yes. That's it, pancakes with lots of chocolate chips."

Matt smiles at me and says, "I do love the chocolate chip pancakes here. They are amazing. But my surgeon has ordered me to pay attention to my diet so if I have pancakes at all; I've been ordered to have the more nutritious multi-grain ones."

"John Pea, may I also have some water and coffee," Looking at Matt, he lets me know with a small nod and lift of his index finger, that he would like coffee too, "A coffee for my date as well," I append. Within a couple of minutes, a pitcher of cream, our coffees, and my water is delivered. Matt drinks coffee also but keeps his black he says he likes it black and bitter. Each to his own, I always say.

John Pea returns to clear our table when we've finished. Suddenly a feeling of deja vu overcomes me. I look at him and ask him, "Do I know you? I could swear we've met..."

"No, ma'am. I'm certain we've not met. I would remember meeting such a lovely woman." John Pea responds. He adds a courteous bow to us both as we stand to leave.

We step outside to a nearby garden. There Matt teaches me to draw the runes we need for travel. He says, "I'll take you to a private place. A place I'm certain no one else has been known to travel. Afterward, I'll return us here. Then, since one can only travel to places one can picture, Shawna, you should then be able to replicate the trip for us both."

"Sounds easy," I mumble back then add, "whatever," under my breath.

Matt takes me, and we come straight back. It was a beautiful place where we were standing on a tall cliff, overlooking a vast sea. It's my turn now. I'm a little scared.

Matt notices and encourages, "My dear Shawna, I'm here with you. You'll be okay, I promise." He presses up against me, and I start to draw my rune on the wall of the garden, near the restaurant where we ate. Before I make the last mark, I look into his eyes, and he looks back. Hell, I can't wait to kiss him. Tearing myself away I concentrate on the place he had shown me a few minutes ago then make my last mark, and we're sucked though.

We arrive deep under a sea of water!

Well, I guess deep is relative. We are at least ten feet deep. As I swim to the surface, I see Matt doing the same. When we reach the top, I take a breath and gasp laughing. Matt reaches the surface with me sputtering and laughing too.

It's warm here. Whoever lives here won't have snow for the holidays. Matt points with his chin to a nearby sandy shore, so we swim to the beach. When we get to a point we can stand and walk, Matt reaches for me, with little effort he pulls me into his arms and carries me the rest of the way to the shore. He lays me down on the wet sand and takes off his shirt to wring it out. After he gets the majority of the water out of it, he hands it to me so I can wipe off some of the water.

I suck in a breath at the sight of his beautiful body. But I catch Matt all but staring at my breasts. Quickly I glance down and notice my wet white tee is all but transparent. I laugh at myself as I watch Matt sit beside me. I lean toward him, meaning to kiss him on the cheek. As I do, he turns just in time for me to catch his lips. Well, thank heaven I don't have to wait and dream of this moment in torture. He kisses me back, soft and gentle, then backs off to see if I liked it. I'm certainly okay with it. So I say, "Thank you for not being afraid to do that. I really like you."

I see he was worried and relaxes at my words then he grabs my waist and rolls over with me on tops of him. He says, "You're the prize, Shawna. Thank you for letting me have the kiss, but next time will you warn me of a dip in the water?" I bat a hand at him, jump up and take off running. He's up quickly, chasing after me. Of course, I let him catch me… after an appropriate pursuit. *What's the fun if I outrun him.* As he catches me, we both topple onto the sand, laughing. After another brief kiss, we relax and lie there together enjoying the moment.

# ANOTHER KISS

The day is playing out more like a dream as my handsome king teaches me a lot about travel. I'm sure now that I can do it alone. I want to know more about him so ask, "Matt what do you shift into? A dragon, like your name implies?"

"Yes, beautiful, I'm a dragon shifter, and my dragon likes you just as much as I do. Would you like to see what I look like in my dragon guise?" He asks.

I'm so shocked that he called me beautiful, my voice comes out low and dreamy sounding, "You bet I do."

He stands and says, "I'm pretty big. Please don't be scared. Are you sure you want to see?"

Pretty sure he didn't mean for me to take those words the way I'm imagining. I answer, "Ready when you are."

He backs away from me as I watch him intently. He's something to look at... then I see a shimmer. Suddenly, in his place is a huge blue and white dragon with golden horns and talons. His wings are up, and I can tell he's posing for me, so I walk over to him. He's as still as a statue while I run a hand over his scaly body. I walk all the way around him, and on an impulse, I put a foot on his bent knee and climb up onto him. He turns to stare at me.

I nod at him and say, "If it won't hurt you, do you mind?"

He swings his head wide and takes off with a mighty leap. The leap slams me closer to him, and I hang on for dear life. *Oh heavens, what was I thinking?* I'm enthralled by the view. In the beginning, his movements are gentle and smooth. *He's taking care with me. I know he won't hurt me, so I enjoy the most beautiful thing ever, flying with my dragon. Uh oh, did I say 'my' dragon? Yes, and I'm really keeping him.* I lean into him and squeeze tighter with my thighs. Those riding lessons as a kid are coming in handy. He lands holding me in place with his great wings. I flip a leg over and slide down until I'm touching the ground. My body is so weak after riding such a powerful beast; I lean into him for balance. After a shimmer, I'm leaning against him, and he's holding me close.

"My lady no one has ever been brave enough to touch my dragon, much less ride him. You've made me the happiest man in any world––ever. Marry me." I start to laugh, but he has the most serious demeanor. I refuse to hurt him, so I conceive of something better to say that won't shame him.

"You are definitely my first pick, but don't you suppose that we should get to know each other before we jump the broom? What if you decide you don't like me?" I make sure I look serious then smile.

He smiles back and says, "Whatever you say my lady, but I'm not changing my mind. Let me know when you're ready. I'll wait for you forever, but I hope you don't make me and… I do love you." Then changing the subject, he says, "Do you want to try your rune travel skills and take us home?"

"Ummm, okay… how do we do that without a wall? Do

we go find one? What if I jump you one way and me another and get lost?"

"I will always find you, I promise. A tree will do, and we have lots of those handy."

"Oh duh," I answer as we walk over to the nearest one. With a glance, I ask if this particular tree is okay.

"Yes beautiful, it is."

I pull the marker he'd given me out of my pocket. As I write the rune, I imagine home. I know it works as we step into the foyer of my mansion home and get sand all over the floor. I'll have to apologize for this as soon as I figure out who to tell.

Matt takes my hands in his and asks, "May I kiss you goodbye?"

Again, I'm speechless. I'm left to stare blankly at him nodding my head. He bends to kiss me. The day just gets better and better. When he stops I sigh loudly for his benefit, and because I act like a schoolgirl around him. He smiles.

"Shawna, may I have the pleasure of accompanying you to dinner in the castle tomorrow?"

I'd love to go with him right now, but I answer, "Yes, I'd love that."

# WHERE AM I

*J*watch Matt as he leaves. When I turn to go upstairs, I spy Howard and Mae watching me. I give them my best 'well what would you do face.' and try to keep a straight face after that. I fail and break out laughing instead. Then we're all laughing uproariously.

I manage, "Howard, I'm so sorry for the floor. If you show me where the vacuum is, I'll clean it up after I have a bath."

"You'll do no such thing. Get your bath, I'll send Jodi to collect your clothes, and I'll keep Miss Mae company until you return. Just ask Jodi to show you to the kitchen when you're ready, if you please, ma'am?"

"Perfect, and Mae I'll be quick. Also, would you have supper with me?"

"Yes, my dear. I'd love to," she answers.

Jodi accompanies me to the kitchen after I'm cleaned up, the smell is so delicious, it's killing me. I'm ready to eat, and they look ready to serve the meal. I sit at a beautiful marble table where Mae is drinking a cup of tea.

I say, "I'm starving, what's for dinner?" Howard proceeds

to order several people to show us our choices. "May I have soup and bread?" They begin serving me immediately."

Mae says, "I'd love soup and bread as well."

We eat the richest potato soup and flakiest croissants ever as we talk like old friends.

"Mae, I believe I have a crush on Esler's king. You know he isn't the ass I thought at first?"

She laughs, "My darling, have you taken the kingdom's most eligible bachelor off the market?" I laugh with her.

"You know Mae, I wonder, is everyone in Elser a shifter? Oh wait, I have to tell you, I got to see the king's dragon today!"

"What? That's amazing. Hardly anyone's seen him as a dragon and yes, we all shift. Would you like to see me shift?"

"Of course, I do," I quip. Do we need to go outside?"

"No here is fine." There's a shimmer, and then a little purple winged pixie is flying in front of my face. She zooms around the kitchen and comes back with a cookie for me.

"Thank you, Mae. Is everyone here as beautiful as you and Matt?"

"Yes, and some, like you, are even more beautiful," she answers as she shifts back into her human form. "I overheard you're invited to the castle tomorrow for dinner. I'm certain you don't know this yet, but you'll need to dress formally for that."

"Wait, what?" I panic.

"It's okay dear. We can go shopping in the morning. I know just the place to get the nicest dress."

"Thank you, Mae. I love the idea."

We finish our meal talking about the dinner tomorrow as well as what to expect. The time comes for her to leave and she draws a rune on the wall near her place at the table. I watch as she quickly disappears in a swirling convection of twisting wall, furniture and Mae. Just as quickly, the wall returns to its normal state, and the rune fades from the wall. I go upstairs, sit on my huge bed, take my chain, and press it then say I want to talk to Anthony. I get his voicemail; can you believe it. Haha, he has a life now! I hope he's as happy as I am, so I leave him a message. I lean back on my bed and fall asleep satisfied and happy.

Someone roughly wakens me from a dead sleep. They flip me over, jerk my hands behind my back, and tie them along with my feet. I try to fight and kick my legs out. I make contact. I hear a loud "Humph," from my assailant. I kick out again and hear a crash as some object in my room hits the floor. I must have missed the dirtbag that time.

Someone rubs lotion on my hands and arms. Suddenly I'm getting dizzy. I feel out of my body. I smell a faint flowery smell as I try to stand to get away, maybe if I shift I can get away. Then I fall, and blackout.

I move to wake and find that I'm not tied up anymore. I'm chained. Looking around to see where I am, I see it couldn't be worse. It's a basement, and I can see what looks like a surgical area on the other side of the room from me. Someone has me shackled to a metal column. I pull and yank the chains. No amount of pulling will loosen the chains grip. I shift into my unicorn shape and find it does no good. My bonds are even tighter and hurt more, so I shift back. I reach for my talk chain and discover it's gone, so I dig into my pockets for my travel marker. It's gone too. Taking a deep breath, I calm myself, so I can devise a plan of escape. My head jerks around to the sound of steps on the stairs. This could be really bad, so I take a defensive stance and watch Jodi walk toward me. I feel so betrayed. I wait in silence forcing her to speak.

"You're a unicorn; I can't kill you. The man I love wants

to marry you so he can claim the estate you robbed from him. Yes, it's okay with me. He loves me not you. And he'll kill or sell you as soon as the deed is signed over to him."

"What! Kill me…"

"What did you think? That we would let you live? You and the king are already making eyes at one another. A dragon and a unicorn would be too powerful for Jeffery to overcome. So, our hand is forced. We must deal with you now."

"You mean my cousin Jeffery?" I ask. The terror of my situation is catching up with me.

"Yes, I mean your cousin Jeffery. He's mine so don't get any ideas. He said he is debating on whether to sell you to prince Barry or kill you later on. If you're very good, and he gets everything he wants, Barry will likely want you after we kill Matt. Then he'll have his brother's throne. He's promised Jeffery and me positions at court.

"You can't escape so don't worry about trying. Jeffery will be here later to get you to sign the family estate over to him. You might consider doing it without a fight. You will marry him. No matter what, your property will fall to him," she says me as she's leaving.

I've looked all over and can't find a way out of this prison. There isn't a window, so I'm not sure what time it is, and they haven't tried to give me any food. I can reach a small sink that is working. I have gotten a drink several times even though the water tastes terrible with a metallic flavor. I do have a small area with a toilet that I have used a couple of times. But I feel strange using it while wondering if someone is watching me.

# HAVE I LOST HER

## MATT

*Y*esterday was so wonderful compared to the last few months. I thought that I would never be able to be happy again since my parents' deaths. I finally see sunshine at the end of the dark tunnel I've been traveling since their deaths. Shawna is a dream come true. They say that if you spend time with a unicorn, you will fall in love in days, but it seems like it only took minutes for me to figure out I love her.

I receive a message notification from my talk chain. Mae wants to speak with me. "Please put her through," I speak into my talk.

"Matt?" I hear her, and she sounds excited in a bad way. I'm immediately worried.

"Yes, Mae, what's wrong?" I ask.

"I'm not sure, Your Highness, may I come to speak with you? It's urgent and concerning Shawna."

"Come right now," I answer turning to my assistant, "Cancel all of my appointments. I'll be in my study with Mae." My assistant Loren is already leaving the room as Mae is popping through the aether. I motion for her to go into my study that we are in front of and she does.

"Mae, would you like something to drink?"

"No, Your Highness, I do need your help. I was supposed to go shopping with our unicorn for a dress this morning. She was so excited to go. She wanted to look perfect for your dinner tonight. But when I arrived to pick her up, I couldn't find her. She isn't at home or anywhere else on the estate. At least not that I can see. Her room looks like there may have been a struggle. I'm afraid that one of the staff at the estate is also missing. A woman named Jodi, she's known to be a friend or maybe more than a friend to Jeffery and Barry, sire."

I'm instantly on guard and turn my attention to her, keeping silent to hear what she has to say.

Your brother Barry, sire, was heard by many people who will vouch that he's been trying to overthrow your reign. He's saying he should be the king of Elser. Now, with a unicorn who's close to the throne, it'll be next to impossible to accomplish. Consider this, if you were the last person seen with Shawna before she disappeared you might be held accountable for not just her disappearance but the murder of her grandparents. You would be put away, and he'll have your throne, easily.

"Heavens Mae you make it sound so so… inevitable and probable. Did you find any clues?"

"No Sire, there's nothing but her bedding in the floor and an overturned lamp from her nightstand." Mae answers.

"I tell the pixie one moment, while I ask my guard at the door, "Find me the wolf shifter Jaxon and have him meet us at Shawna Rollins's mansion in the woods."

"Mae, the wolf is the best tracker in our army. Let's go so I can have a look. Even if she weren't the girl I've been searching for the whole of my life, she's a part of this king-dom, a unicorn, and able to help us like no other can." *I must find her. I may not wish to survive if I don't.* Right now, I'm holding my anger, but I can feel it boiling up inside.

Mae, with a worried frown, draws a travel rune on the wall and we arrive in Shawna's bedroom. I do a partial shift into my dragon form and sniff the entire room. I know that Barry was here and touched her bed covers. A roar builds, and I release it in a booming burst when I smell some of my unicorn's blood. It isn't much, maybe just a scratch, but that is more than enough to make my temper flare red hot.

I tell my pixie friend, "It's obvious that there was a struggle here and someone cut her enough that I can smell her blood. They used a drug I'm only vaguely familiar with. I understand it's equal to a roofie from the Earth realm." I finish as Jaxon travels into the room. I inform him what I believe to have happened and he shifts into a huge wolf and stalks around the room. He stops in front of me and tells me telepathically to follow him. The telepathy is a dragon king gift. Anyone of my subjects who knows how to speak this way can speak to me in our minds if I allow it. My army and soldiers are always able. He walks toward the door of the room, and I motion with my head to Mae to follow. He stops when he gets to the front foyer and says this is the room that they traveled from then the soldier points to a spot on the wall where Mae sprinkles some magic and the rune shows up. We retrace the rune and travel finding ourselves in the middle of the forest.

Jaxon sniffs out a trail to an old fallen tree. The smell is so strong of something dead that we can hardly smell the trail. There is a body of a deceased person in the tree. Jaxon does find them, but the scent trail ends in the air. Someone flew off with her. He shifts and says, "Sire, I'll keep looking and send the scent to my pack mates, but for now this is as far as I can get you."

I roar and fly up into the sky in a rage. It takes a lot to shoot fire like a dragon but right now I need an outlet and let the fire blow from my anger. When my mind clears, I return to the castle where I find the search for Shawna is in full progress. I've nothing to do now but wait. Waiting isn't easy for me. I hate the feeling. I promised to find her if she's lost, and that's what I'm going to do.

# I FIGURE IT OUT

$\mathcal{I}$'ve tried everything and don't have any idea how to get loose, so I fall asleep. I dream of my handsome lover and discover he has my dragons face. I thought Matt was familiar. Oh, that makes me very happy. Even in my dream, I remember that I'm a prisoner. Like my subconscious, my unicorn self starts telling me how to get out of the basement. I only hope I remember it when I wake.

*"Shawna you can escape. However, you must stay hidden after you do. Peter, Jodi, and Barry must be dealt with before you return to the castle. Also, the people need to know who I am."*

I wake so I can get out before I'm forced to marry my cousin. I concentrate on the feelings I had when I faded upon meeting the king for the first time. I let the fear and desperation fill me, but this time I have it controlled. As I concentrate I fade, just like I did that day.

I'm now entirely invisible and have no substance. The chains drop from me to the floor with a clang. *Oops, I hope no one heard that. I better scoot just in case.* I quietly walk up the steps and phase through the door. I'm not solid, not flesh, right now. I'm in a kitchen where there's an outside door. Again, I phase through it and walk out into the cold morning air.

Panic takes hold, and I run. As I start, I notice that I'm in a city much like a downtown area of an Earth city. *Wait for a second.* I need to know where the building I was held is. I must be able to find it again, so they can't do this to others. It is a business and has a sign that says Mart Brother's Laundry.

I won't forget. I start running again and don't stop until I'm well out of the city and can only see a few homes on the edge of a large lake. A lake that has fisherman in boats with ice chunks floating around the murky water. There's a group of seals at the water's edge. I slowly walk toward them, and they let me. They can see me. I must have let the invisibility go once I was out of danger. I'm thirsty from my run, but no way am I drinking that filthy water. I can't believe the seals have been in the disgusting sliminess. I remember faintly that someone told me that a unicorn could clean up water, so I put my horn into the water. I remember reading a story once that a unicorn's horn had cleaned up a pool with poison in it. Well, it can't hurt to try. I walk into the water just a few steps and dip my horn in and instantly the water around it turns blue and crystal clear. Then I stir it around a little, and the gentle waves carry the effect through the entire lake. I take a deep drink and satisfy my parched throat. When I step back, I see the seals are all shifted into a group of people who are bowing to me.

One rises and says, "Thank you, gentle unicorn. We've needed that for more years than I can count. Now the fish can flourish again, and the circle of life will continue."

Immediately, I shift back into my human form and smile at them.

"What can we do to return the favor, my lady?"

"Well, first I need everyone here to keep the secret of what you've just witnessed including the men in the boats. Can someone beg them for their confidence?"

Without hesitation one of the men shifts back into a seal and swims to the first boat. After speaking to the man in the boat, the man looks to me and tips his hat. Then, the same seal is off to the next boat.

"That's wonderful! I'm hungry too so is there a place where I can get something to eat and rest. I need to figure out what to do to get home."

"Come with us, my lady. My name is Rick, and this is my family. We will take you to my home. You understand that others will see that the water is clean. Even if we keep your secret, we can't hide that?" The seal spokesman says.

"Yes, that's true, let's go quickly. I need to keep hidden. I'll tell you my story and see if we can work a deal so that I can get home and pay you back."

They take me to a beautiful cottage where the water is only yards from the door. As I enter, I feel the hominess and warmth. The smell of fresh bread baking hits me. Rick seats me at a long table and introduces his wife Amy and his daughter Kelly along with his son they call li'l Robert. I find it interesting they call him that because 'li'l Robert' is humungous!

Amy has a plate of food in front of me in no time and a large tankard of ale. Kelly is so shy she just sits and stares at me. Robert is bringing in wood for the fireplace and has it started in just a couple of minutes. I tell them my story. In my gut, I know that I can trust these people. Rick is calm but decisive when I finish.

He says, "My brother is in the king's army. With your approval, I'll contact him and see what he wants to do."

I nod my approval. Rick quickly stands and marks a rune on the wall. In less than a minute, he returns.

"I spoke with my brother. He feels it would be safer if you stay hidden here with us. His understanding is that it will allow the king to take care of the criminals who abducted you. He has also already sent a message to the King. We should hear something soon."

True to his word, in a matter of seconds we receive this message from the king.

---

Hello my beautiful, Shawna,

I'm relieved beyond measure that you're safe. Please stay where you are for the next few days. I know and trust this family completely. I miss you and long to hold you again soon.

Unwaveringly yours,

Matt

---

WITH THAT WEIGHT LIFTED, WE SPEND THE REST OF THE NIGHT telling stories in front of the fire. I eventually drift off sitting in my chair.

I know I'm asleep, so I seek my magical dream lover. As soon as I search, he's there in front of me. He says, "That was such a brave thing you did to escape my bold girl. Shawna, are you alright, really?"

"Yes, love, I am."

"I want to come to you, but that will surely bring our enemies and trouble to you. I don't want to ever risk losing you again." He reaches for me, and I sink into him. No wonder I have an instant attraction for Matt I've known him for years in my dreams.

I whisper," I trust you and will wait, however impatiently. I want you here. Can you take care of them fast, my love?" I show him a memory of what Mart's Brothers Laundry looked like from the outside. Then I say, "I'm with a kind family of seals just off the waterfront." I laugh at my minor humor.

I hear him laugh in return. It is luxurious. "For you, anything. I'll resolve this as fast as I can." He rocks me, and I fall deeper into sleep.

# HIDING OUT

*A* hand is on my shoulder shaking me awake. Unicorn Shawna, you must not be flesh when the king's brother gets here. They can't track you when you are an invisible unicorn. You will have no scent, they will not even be able to see tracks from your passing. I look at Amy, and with a quick nod I change. She's put a saddlebag full of food and water over my back and holds the back door open for me saying she will see me again. I leave and head into the woods a few feet then disappear when I look back to be sure they are safe I see them all sneaking out the opposite way that I ran, several bags in each of their hands.

In seconds I hear the booming, thunderous sound of a dragon threatening the home. It must be Barry. I'm petrified and stand frozen in my spot. He's as huge as Matt but much uglier, and he is pissed. He continues to yell at the house from the sky.

I see Jodi, and a man I would guess is cousin Jeffery come out the back door of the seal family's home. I'm close enough that I hear them say that no one is there, and the scent of the unicorn is gone. I hold my breath. It is so hot now, with my heart beating out of my chest. I watch them leave. In moments the whole house has burst into flames. Barry is burning my friends home. My heart sinks. Bile rises in my throat. *I will find them and repay them as soon as I can.* Running to get the heck out of here before they find me I feel scared for my friends. The day is cool but not the wintery bluster that yesterday was. Keeping a steady trot keeps me warm, but I really have to rest. Still invisible I find a big stand of trees that are close together and lie down in the middle where the bushes are thickest and have just enough room for me to get behind. It isn't long when I hear hounds barking and wake with a jerk. Again, I'm frozen in place. *What should I do so they won't find me. I'm still invisible. If it is true that I have no scent how are the hounds finding me? It might be the food in my saddle bags that they smell.* I take them off and hang it in the tree. *I'll come back for it if I don't find anything else.* When I run away, I hear that the dogs have become much louder and frenzied in their barking. I hold still and listen. A cold chill runs down my back. My heart is beating out of my chest again. Barry in his dragon form passes me so close that I almost want cry. A warm sulfurous breeze hits me in his wake. I was right about the guy I called the reaper. He's bad. He's prince Barry. I'm sure that he doesn't know I'm here. The asshat gets closer to the dogs. Jodi, I knew she was a dog, shifts and Barry shifts at the same time. Jeffery who must also be one of the dogs also shifts. That's so perfect in my mind he and Jodi are dog shifters.

They stand and talk saying that the trail is lost, and they will go back to town to see if they can find someone who they can pay to track the blasted unicorn. This time when they catch me, they will kill me and save themselves more trouble.

When they all have left, I take a deep breath and relax my stiff muscles only a little. I have to get out of this forest. I start walking on tip hooves as quietly as possible, and trip over an old fire pit. I hear the noise, but the birds don't even fly or stop chirping. While on the ground I see the burned coals of a long-dead fire and have an idea. Picking through the coals, I find one that I surmise will work and write a travel rune on the nearest tree then picture the beach where Matt had taken me. In a twinkling, I'm there and still invisible with the burnt coal in hand.

It's time for me to experiment a little. I change into my woman shape, but stay invisible. I was able to keep up the invisibility even while I slept so I believe this will work if I just do not materialize. I walk into the water and wash off all the day's dirt and wash out my clothes. I hang the wet clothes on a bush a few yards from the beach. Then I lie down on the soft, warm sand and dry off. I never hear anyone or see anyone, and I'm not panicked anymore. This might just be the ticket. Matt will find me I'm sure he will remember this place when he has caught the ones trying to kill me. I'll just pop into shops in the Earth realm to get food and maybe a blanket and towel. Wow, what a terrible idea. I'll go to my house there on Earth. I need to talk to Anthony anyway. I draw a rune and am on my way.

# GETTING SUPPLIES

*J*pop right into the living room, startling Anthony. He's sitting on the couch with an open book which he promptly drops from his hands. It is obvious I've shocked my longtime friend. His mouth falls open and remains that way.

"Oh hey, Anthony... I mean, hi honey, I'm home," I say with a smile. I pause for a couple of long breaths. When he doesn't speak, I continue "Honey, the weirdest things have been happening. I need to tell you about them. If you have a few minutes." I laugh as I finish, hoping to add some levity to the room. It didn't work.

"Freaking firetruck, Ro! Tell me how you just showed up out of thin air! Did I miss something? I promise I'm totally sober."

"You have missed a bunch. I believe you're sober. Aaannnd, I'll share everything if you will pretty please with chocolate on top, get me a cup of coffee. Oh, are you off work today?"

Anthony stands, just a bit nervously, and goes to pour me

a steamy cup of brew. When he hands it to me, he says, "Yes, I'm off early. A truck hit an electrical pole up the street from the office. I guess the driver thought she was an ice skater. Anyway, she took out the power for several blocks."

"Anthony, sweetheart, you always know how to make life fun. Anyway, I'll bet it was a male driver," I retort. Anthony and I have always teased each other over which gender was the better driver. I point to the insurance statistics. He doesn't know how to admit defeat.

"Sit down, Ro. You look like you've fought a gargoyle... and lost. Roja, why do you look so run down and how in the holy transporter did you pop in like that."

We sit down, and I relate what has happened. Everything that I've been through and leave out nothing. Not even the part where I've found the greatest guy and have already fallen for him. It must be dragon magic. When I finish my whole story, Anthony hugs me and says that he believes me. That is so important to me. I was afraid that he would judge that I've gone off the deep end.

Then with a look like a light bulb just went off he says, "So do you expect that if you stay in Elser you can be invisible, and no one will find you for sure?"

"Yes, I'm sure that they can find me here, given time, and relatively sure they can't there as long as I stay invisible. Can we order a pizza or something? I'm starving."

"Yes, I'll order." He says picking up his phone. "While we wait for pizza I want to get some stuff for you from the shed. You can shower and pack clothes while I'm outside."

He got a small tent, an air mattress, sleeping bag, and a whole pile of stuff that I might need and stacked it in the living room floor.

"Now show me where we're going," he says.

"Okay, but I have to be invisible so don't be shocked

when we get there, and you can't see me. I'll bump you if you can't hear me. In fact, this'll be a good time to learn more about what I can and can't do when I'm invisible." I get a marker out of my room so I can mark the travel rune.

We both grab as much as we can carry and are just able to bring it all. As I mark the rune, I prepare him for what will happen. We arrive safely. On land even, I count as another win. Yay, a great takeaway! We spend the rest of the day camouflaging a little camp area in the trees off the beach. I stay invisible and find that he can hear me, all I had to do was aim to make it so he can.

When we finish I take him back home and say, "Anthony, I don't mind if you want to live with me at the mansion in the forest."

"Thank you dear, but I have Don, and we're starting to conclude we're long-term, he says.

"Oh, I'm happy for you both. You know that I only want the best for you. If you change your mind, you are more than welcome. I'll try to pop in often and say hello. Only next time I'll come in through my bedroom. I wouldn't want to scare any of your guests."

Laughing Anthony responds, "Probably a good idea. I couldn't imagine trying to explain this to other people."

"Anthony…," I pause because this is hard for me, "we have been together for most of our lives. It might be a while before we get to see each other again. I don't know what is going on right now. If you need to tell me something, leave me a note on my bed. It might be late, but I'll get it."

I take him home and give my friend a big hug. I feel like crying and laughing at the same time. I know that I want to live in Elser now. I want Matt. *I'm going to take a chance and be bold;* then I travel back alone. I search around my little-hidden camp, and I see no sign that anyone is anywhere around. So tomorrow I'll take a run. Then I'll take another in the other direction. I'll keep doing this until I can make out a quick map of the area. Well, at least it's a plan.

The next morning, I'm up bright and early and start running east. I've gone quite a ways, it takes me several hours when I leave the edge of the forest and transition into a field of plants about four feet tall. I see a few workers harvesting pineapples, so I concentrate on being sure that I'm not visible and sound free. They're wearing thick coarse one-piece suits with long sleeves, hats, and gloves. Each of them has a long knife, and they are very good at cutting the ripe fruit and putting in on a conveyor belt that leads up to a truck bed. There are a couple of workers in the truck who are gathering the fruit and putting it gently in rows.

It's fascinating to watch, and I stand and watch for a while. I hear one of the gatherers ask, "Do you notice the plants over there." The worker is pointing straight at me. I briefly panic until I hear him continue. "Those plants look a lot better than the rest." I watch as they bow their heads respectfully and then I hear the same man say with a giant sigh, "It must be a unicorn."

*Wait! What? How could he possibly know?* Then I see what he's talking about. The square plot of plants where I'd walked and now stand, look much greener and appear ready to bear fruit again. They look very much unlike the wilted plants covering the rest of the field. A little panic creeps in as I recognize that once again, I must ask people I don't know to help protect me.

I get close to them and let them hear me. I beg, "Will you please keep my presence a secret? I'm being hunted by some bad men."

One and all tip their heads down and one says, "We wish

you to maintain your presence here, gentle unicorn. Please stay, we will tell no one."

Once again, the people of Elser risk their safety to protect mine. I'm so happy that a little musical note comes from my horn when I huff air as I relax. How embarrassing, I feel like I just farted in church. They, on the other hand, are so happy they all laugh and start harvesting again.

I revert to my stealth mode. I'm calling it silent but deadly. I laugh out loud at my own joke. I realize, in a most intrinsic way, I love living this life. Who would've thought I would be so bold and brave while still being scared of my own shadow!

I find my way back to my tent by nightfall and sit alone pondering. The island is bigger than I had initially believed. My thoughts run from one subject to another with no real logic behind them. The one consistency is when I'm able I want to help the people here someway. Their welfare will be my mission.

I fall fast asleep. Then I dream.

"Matt are you here," I say into my dreamscape. He walks straight up to me and puts his hands on my waist pulling me into his broad muscular chest. He is shaking. I push into him, and we are touching from knee to chest, trying to comfort him. My head leaning into him I say, "I'm alright, Matt, and safe. Are you all right?"

"I was afraid for you. I'll be fine now that I know you're safe. When we found the burned cottage, I was frightened that you hadn't made it out before the dragon fire. We have just found my brother and your cousin in their hideout. The army and I will be marching on them tomorrow."

Now I'm the one afraid for him. He says, "My love, I'll be safe. I'll come to you as soon as this is over. Before that, though, I need to ensure the criminals are dealt with. If they go peaceably, they'll be imprisoned where there is no hope of escape. They can't be permitted to hurt you in this way ever again."

"Matt don't worry about me. While I'm invisible, I can't be tracked by scent or sound."

"Very good. I'm impressed you've learned so much so quickly. Here's something more for you to know. It is normal for a dragon king to be able to speak to his subjects telepathically, but what we have in dreams is only heard of in ancient manuscripts and only in situations where the two are deeply in love."

Odd that I don't blush. His information doesn't surprise me. We share for a little while longer, and he kisses me sweetly. "My love, get some rest. Stay hidden, and I'll see you tomorrow--in the flesh.

# THE BATTLE

## MATT

*I* awake at 0400 to finalize the plan with my general. They believe they have the power to complete the mission without me. "Highness, we will accomplish this mission. We had hoped that you would remain home, away from the danger."

"General Wolf, I know you believe what you're saying. Don't be fooled though, only a dragon can subdue another dragon. For this reason alone, I'll participate in this attack. Just in case you forget, my good general, what they did to my lady unicorn... I take it personally. I'll attend to their punishment. I can't place her in further jeopardy by failing in my responsibility to do everything in my power to bring her captors to justice."

During the night, General Wolf placed his troops like chess pieces on a board. By morning the nondescript house in the middle of the forest where Barry, Jeffery, and Shawna's former maid, Jodi are hiding is completely surrounded. At least as entirely as ground forces can make it. Throughout the night, my general had ordered red fireballs shot into the air at odd intervals. These red fireballs were immediately followed by blue fireballs showing the precise location of the criminals to the army and give commands understood only by the Elser army.

To further hinder any possible escape, the Royal Wizard, Jatter the Hart, placed a magical dampening spell around the perimeter of the building at twenty plus eleven paces. Due to the exceedingly complex nature of this type of magic, it can only be accomplished by those who have attained a mastery of wizardry. I'm glad I have his loyalty. There are only two, or possibly, three shifters in the entire kingdom which can perform such a spell. I have the utmost confidence that my army will capture two of the three criminals. Barry, my brother, however, is as clever as any and stronger than all but me. I won't let him escape today.

General Wolf asks, "My king, are you ready to proceed?"

I nod my answer as a red fireball shoots into the sky. After a count of three, the blue fireball is sent. This is the command to proceed. The army advances, the circle of fighters, men and women alike, tighten like a snake around its prey.

I'm moving at a much slower pace than the army and keep my distance in preparation for preventing my brother Barry's escape. I need to try to keep him from getting too hurt in the process.

The army halts and a herald demands, "All creatures, fae or human are hereby ordered to exit this building and present themselves for judicial complaint. Any resistance will be assumed to be an admission of guilt."

As if on cue the door swings open and Barry, Jeffery, and Jodi step from the building with their hands held high in the cold morning air.

General Wolf commands, "Arrest team, move in." Twelve

of the largest men and women move in. Six are in human form, and six are in various forms of large animals. As the humans take hold of the three criminals, Barry throws something directly at me and the world goes black as I pass out. After a time, the black turns to grey then the colors slowly return to my vision. I notice that I'm sitting upright. On first sight, after the blackout, I spot an entire regiment of my army lying on the ground--unmoving. Gasping, I recognize that I've lost twenty-five percent of the army with one device thrown by Barry.

I yell, "Jatter! Where are you?"

"I'm here, my king," the wizard answers.

"What was that thing that my brother threw at us and where is general Wolf?" I ask.

"Sire, it was a concussion stunner spell."

"Jatter, you had a magical barrier up..." I let the words trail off without actually asking any question. The stunner effect is still affecting me.

"Yes, sire. The barrier did prevent any transformation, or any magical spells being cast. Somehow your brother found a way to hold a previously cast spell in a containment vessel. When he threw the container, and it ruptured, no spell was cast. But the effect was the same."

"Do you mean he can carry spells with him?"

"The obvious answer is yes. Yet, that only tells part of the story. It's unlikely he can carry more than one. He likely cast this spell just before I invoked the barrier. If we would have waited for even another ten marks the spell would have weakened significantly."

"Jatter, where are the criminals?"

"My king I can only speak regarding Jeffery and the maid Jodie. They are holed up in the nearby Ryukyuan Cave system. The Shishi gargoyle clan holds that territory by royal decree. We have sent an emissary to Komainu, their king, to request assistance. We're sure to have an answer at any moment."

"Where is Barry?"

"He's fled, Your Highness."

My mind is racing. Where has my brother gone? He's one who will always take the initiative. He will attempt to find Shawna. If he can see her, he may believe he can still win... but where? Then it hits me. "Shawna's a unicorn!" I yell.

"Highness?" Jatter asks.

"Jatter, I have no time. I must leave, now! You and the general must convince Komainu to take hold of the fugitives and return them to your custody. Jatter listens closely. Under no circumstances can these two escape. Do you understand me?"

"Yes, sire."

Now that I'm confident the wizard understands the implied requirements of my order I feel free to leave and capture Barry. I quickly mark my travel rune on the nearest tree and take off traveling to the location where Shawna must be... on the island. Upon arrival, I transform into my dragon self and leap into the sky searching for Barry and any ground signs of my lovely unicorn. I'm looking for anything at all that she's been in the area.

In a flash, I find the unicorn's sign all over the island. Lush greenery is growing in paths and leads back to the beach. This is where I finally figure out that Shawna has got to be hidden. I want to warn her but can't because I must stop Barry, here and now, before he also discovers her. I fly over in a patrol to the end of the unicorn signs and am rewarded when I see Barry flying below me.

He has never looked so awful. It seems that his hide is matching his character and it's ugly. I dive down and catch him in an attempt to hold him trying to remember that he's my younger brother and I don't wish him harm. Yet, my dragon brother seems to feel no such restriction and yells at me, "Brother, abdicate the throne. I'll let you both live in peace on this island where I know the unicorn is in hiding. It's the most magical place in the realm, she must be here. I just have to find where."

"No brother, I will not abdicate, and I won't help you find the unicorn. I can't trust that you will let her live." I'm praying she's on the other side of the island, at our beach, and stays there.

Barry cuts at me with his talons. One of the only things that can cut a dragon is another dragon. I flinch then recover. I can't afford to let him go, he's too dangerous. Tightening my grip, Barry turns like a vicious cat and rakes my body from head to foot. I'm bleeding badly and break free. My brother turns on me and ignites his dragon fire. A large spray of fire bursts forward, just missing me, then he rushes toward me again.

I shout, "Barry, you know I'm the stronger of us, and I will not let you win!"

"Rrrroooaarrr aaarrrrggghhh!" The sound was both pained and angry simultaneously. Barry races toward me flying as fast as he can. To him, this is an all or nothing gambit, and it's too late to try to convince him otherwise. I, however, am here just in time to deal with him. Barry collides with me again. I grab onto him using my talons this time to dig deep into him and hold him tightly. We start to fall to the ground unable to fly we are so wrapped up together. There's nothing left for me to do that would help avoid the consequences of my baby brother's criminal behavior. Memories of our childhood flash through my mind. Somehow, only the excellent and glorious though. The ground rises toward us. I remember that we loved to fly across the ocean to the lands of our ancestors. We crash into the sand, and there is a sickening crunch as my brother's neck breaks on impact. Barry is dying. I gather him close into my great dragon arms. He has no strength left and shifts into his man shape. I shift with him. My anger gone, crashed in a great heap on the ground with us. Now all I have left of my baby brother is dying in my arms, and it pains me to the quick.

I beg, "Hold on Barry. I called for a healer. They'll be here, and you can live. She'll be here soon. I've also called to Shawna; the unicorn can save you too. Please brother hold on." We had flown further than I had thought and now a delay is the result.

"I'm sorry brother, I do love…" Barry says, and then he's gone.

My sorrow comes out in a full roar as I vent my pain into the surrounding air. Suddenly spent, I'm drained of all energy. The flow of blood from my wounds has not abated, and I murmur to Barry's still corpse, "Brother, it seems I might join you in death."

# I WAIT

$\mathcal{I}$ travel around as much of the island as I can today. I recognize the best way to help the people here who are keeping me safe is by making the area thrive. That is what I do, so I walk everywhere. Flowers bloom wherever I've been. I'm trying to keep busy and not worry about what Matt is doing and whether he's safe or not. I know he'll return to me as soon as this mess is ended. It's taking way too long. I'll be ecstatic when this ordeal is over, and I can get back to my own little, I mean a vast mansion and relax. I want Matt with me and really must quit daydreaming about him. It's making the wait torturous.

I'm in the middle of a forested area when I hear crying, so I move toward the noise. It's a child, a little girl alone. She looks maybe seven or eight years old. As I walk over to her, I shed my invisibility. Now she can see me as a human. With all that I have, I hope that Matt has already taken care of our problems and I'm not endangering myself or him by being seen. Still, I can't let this little one sit here and cry and not help. She's obviously lost. I sit beside her and say, "Hi there, my name is Shawna. What's yours?"

She looks up at me with big tear-filled eyes and gulps a little then answer, "My name's Patti, and I lost my mommy!" This statement has her wailing again and crawling into my lap.

I wrap my arms around her and say, "We'll just have to go find her then Patti. Do you know where you lost her?"

"In the pineapples," she boo hoos.

"That's a place that I happen to know. Would you like a ride on my back while I walk to the pineapple field?" I ask her.

She nods her head giving me a little smile. I put her on my back and warn her that I'm going to shift. She's okay with it, so I shift and start off to the fields. They're not too far away, so it is only a matter of minutes before we find a group of frantic adults. When they see me, a woman comes running to me with another young girl. The woman takes her daughter off my back, she hugs her, and rocks her back and forth, then she looks over to me and says, "I can't thank you enough. We thought she was with us the whole time. Then when we started to leave, we found that she was gone. We have been searching for at least an hour. A man in his twenties who looks very much like the little girls joins the two of them and takes his little Patti.

"Patti, I'm so glad to have you back. Please, my daughter, don't wander off from us again. Next time, there may not be a unicorn around to find you." Then looking up to me he adds, "I can never thank you enough, gentle unicorn. My name is Teric, this is my wife Erin, and daughter Maddie, and you know Patti already. What can I do to serve you?"

"My name is Shawna, and I'm fine. I don't need anything. Though, it would be helpful if you wouldn't tell anyone about me being here. I'm hiding from some people who are trying to kill me. I will not be on the island for much longer, but if you need me, I'll be close to the beach. I have to leave now. Patti, you stay close to your parents now, okay?" I nuzzle her with my nose and wave to her sister Maddie as I leave.

"Gentle unicorn, Shawna, we're here and will help you also. If you find yourself in need of any assistance, be it protection or even supplies, make your way to the village on the other side of this field and ask for me," Teric informs.

I nod and disappear again and head to my camp so Matt can find me when he's ready. I've been sitting here reading the book Anthony had packed for me. But my mind isn't on it, and I find myself reading the same page and still not knowing what's even written in it. I'm going to the Earth realm to get a hot shower and a cup of coffee with Anthony. Luckily, he's at home, and I fill him in on the murderous trio who are after me. He tells me all about Don.

Hours later, after I'm all caught up with my bestie, I go back to my beach and lay in the warm shaded sand to take a nap and wait for Matt. I just feel off... like something's wrong. The waves rolling in and the active twittering of the birds and other animals help relax me. Also, I might find Matt hiding in my dreams. As I rest, my mind wanders around all of the topics which are keeping me awake. Why hasn't Matt found me yet? Where is he? Is he safe? Am I safe...

Sleep finally catches me. Again, I rule my dreams. "Matt. Matt! Where are you? Matt, are you safe?" I call out to him over and over. I only hear a moan in return for my efforts. My dream self panics. I awaken and jump up. In my human form but still invisible, I grab my marker and put on my shoes. I write my travel rune on the nearest tree, concentrating on the palace. Since I only remember the beautiful gardens, that's where I arrive. I remain invisible as I walk to the palace doors. Here I find a magical spell forces me to become fully human and visible before I can open them.

A guard is standing at the entrance. I touch him with my horn and tell him to let me in to see the king. The dashing guard's eyes are glassy, and his movements become mechanical. He opens the doors without question and holds them until I'm through. Then he closes and secures the doors behind me before returning to his guard station without even the slightest hint that I have passed.

Now that I'm in here I still don't know where to go. I find the wizard who was beside Matt when I first came to Elser, so I follow him. I follow him through the brightly lit passageway, up to a flight of beautifully carved stone stairs, into another wing, and then up another etched flight of stairs. I feel the mere idea of being lost beginning to press its weight onto my shoulders. *Well, Shawna, you can always keep looking around. It isn't like you'll be stuck here... I hope. I'll just follow the sorcerer to his destination regardless of the outcome.* Finally, near the middle of the eastern passageway on the third floor, the mage turns and enters through a large set of doors, each carved with a different gargoyle. I smile to myself speculating, gargoyles are protectors. I follow him into a bedroom.

Oh, heavens no! Matt is a bloody mess. He's lying in the middle of a large bed in the elaborately decorated room. Shock grabs me and shakes me into my visible human form. I rush toward him to hold him and tell him I love him, but as I near his bed, the guards seize me.

I hear Jatter loudly chastise them, "Do you not recognize your unicorn, Shawna?" Then he says, "My lady, he's just arrived from the battle and had surgery to close his wounds. I know it looks terrible. Please sit over here. I won't make you leave, but we must get him cleaned up and change his bedding and bandages. Do you wish to stay?

"Yes, nothing can make me leave him," I answer.

The guards, properly chastised and also chagrined at not recognizing me, had immediately let me go and apologize as they retreat to their station. I reach Matt and touch the only part of him not bloodied, his forehead. Seeing no response, I lean forward and say, "Matt you must fight. Fight with all you have. You must stay alive. I'm going to get you some help. Stay with me, okay, just stay with me."

I shift into my unicorn self and touch my horn to his body. Nothing happens! I touch him everywhere and still nothing. Oh no, what do I do? I'm a failure at being a unicorn. If I just knew what to do and was not so new to my own magic!

# ALL BETTER OR NOT

*J*atter and I sit in two large baroque throne-like chairs next to the window in Matt's room. The velvety blue chairs were amazingly comfortable. Yet it felt like mine had rocks in the seat which were encouraging me to stand and… sit down only to be up again. I sit again.

Jatter shares, "Shawna, the battle between Matt and Barry was one of a king fighting a rival for his throne and in defense of his intended. Matt didn't want to hurt his brother, but Barry felt he must destroy his competition in order to gain the throne. He did significant damage with his talons before the king ended the fight. Matt didn't seek this outcome. Barry broke his neck in a fall during the fight."

I audibly gasp, and my hands lift to cover my gaping mouth. "Oh my, Matt must feel horrible. I'm sure he loves his brother."

"Yes," Jatter continues. "He loves him dearly. Yet, for the sake of his people, for the sake of himself, and for the sake of… you," Jatter pauses a heartbeat and looks directly, what feels like, into my soul before continuing, "he had to destroy Barry. You should also know your cousin Jeffery and Jodi are in prison awaiting their respective trials."

"Jatter," I ask, "how is Matt?"

"Honestly, Matt is in a healing coma. I don't know if he'll recover or not. He's lost his brother, that will affect him. I just don't know. He's lost a lot of blood. We believe the blood loss was between fifty and fifty-five percent. Most patients cannot survive with such a significant loss of blood. Still, if it weren't for the rapid response of the emergency professionals, carrying his blood type with them, Matt would have had a heart attack or worse there in the forest. The rune travel allowed the EP's to return him to the castle as soon as the blood supply was injecting. Were it not for those measures, he could not have survived.

During the surgery, all of his blood was replaced, and all of his wounds were closed. I know of absolutely nothing else to do but wait by his bedside. That is just what we're doing now."

Now that it's getting dark I ask, "Jatter may I stay the night? I really need to stay. I can't leave him."

"I believe that will be helpful. Matt was full of joy when he spoke of you. I believe you may help him rest and recover faster."

I remain by his bedside most of the night. I touch him with my horn again and still nothing. In the morning, the housekeeper changes my dragon's linens, the doctors return to change his bandages, and examine him. In the end, they only nod in sadness and say, "It's up to Matt now." They reassure me that my presence is a good thing and have breakfast sent in to me.

I finish my meal then get up to use the bathroom. *I could use a shower.* I request one of the guards to send for a steward who I ask to travel to my mansion and get me a change of clothing. He does so and returns in only a few minutes. I take a shower and dress. Although, I feel better being freshly bathed and in clean clothing, I'm forcing myself to go through the motions. I only want to hurry back to my dragon.

As bloody as he looked when I first arrived, he seems much better now that he's all cleaned up and has clean sheets. I can't help myself as I lean over him. I feel so low that I can hardly function. When the tears fall they come without warning or release. I cry, "Matt, please get better. What can I do? I'll help if there is anything, anything at all." The tears are now pouring down my chin. I feel bad when I notice that a few tears have fallen on his bandages. Unwilling to cause further problems with a potential infection, I back away. I drop into my chair and move as close to him as I can, then take his hand.

I lay my head with his on his pillow and begin telling him a story. "On Earth, some doctors advise us to talk to people in a coma. So that's what I'm going to do. I know a story of another dragon. A young woman named Iza and her monster, Phobe."

I finish my long story, and my butt is now fast asleep. It's buzzing like my pants are full of bees. The bees demanding I shift positions, I lean away from Matt, but as I pull away, he latches on to my hand.

"Matt," I cry out with hope, "hey dragon, wake up I need to see you."

He opens his eyes and groans low in his throat, "Friend, you're here. Please, don't leave."

"I'm not leaving––ever. You'll have to force me to leave if you want me gone." I motion for a guard and ask, "Will you please get Jatter and the doctors. Alert them that your king is awake."

"Good," Matt says and slips into slumber.

When the doctors and Jatter run into the room, they swarm the king. I move out of their way to let them in close. As I walk away, Matt opens his eyes again and says, "What did you do with my unicorn, I need her." Unable to stay awake he drifts off to sleep again.

I'm so happy now that my heart is full. I need to call Anthony. I need to tell him about Matt. I ask the steward who'd helped me earlier, "May I please get a talk chain to use?" He returns with a brand new one still in the box. As he removes it, he asks, "Is this one good enough?"

I laugh and exclaim, "It's perfect. Also, where can I have a little privacy for my call?" He leads me to a library where I sit and proceed to call my best friend and relate my happy news.

Anthony has news of his own. "I'd like Don to move in to save money for us both. Do you mind?"

"My friend… my best friend forever… this is a good day for good news. Tomorrow, I'll have my solicitors gift you the house."

Anthony has always supported himself. He doesn't like 'charity.' But after I inform him what I get for a monthly check, he accepts. "Shawna, I will love you always."

I knew that already.

# HAPPILY EVER AFTER

$\mathcal{Y}$ears later...

I WAKE FROM AN EXHAUSTED SLEEP TO THE MOST BEAUTIFUL site. My handsome dragon rocking our newborn daughter in his arms singing her a nursery rhyme. Our two sons are asleep lying against me. Having been away for the birth of their sister they need some cuddles.

Matt notices that I'm awake and says, "She is the most beautiful little thing, my darling queen. Thank you, I love you. How are you feeling?"

"Absolutely and totally happy with life. I love you too!"

I'd never have guessed that my life would've turned out this way. Seven years after I stepped into the unknown I'm married to the man of my dreams, literally. I have my beautiful children. We will not really know until it happens, but we sense that our oldest son, Kyle, is a unicorn and will take after me and that our son, Chris, is a dragon like his father. Our little miss Katherine we are pretty sure by the roar at birth is also a dragon. We think we know... but things can change. We thought we were the flesh and bold, but these kids... this is going to be interesting for sure.

The End

# ACKNOWLEDGMENTS

Miki - Thank you, our Fans and Readers. I appreciate each and every one of you. You are my prize. All the members of Miki & Mine who keep me going.

Thank you, Zoe Parker, and all the authors of Shifting Destiny for including us in your anthology it is an honor.

My family, especially Shawna, Patti, and everyone who is always supportive and helpful. My husband, I love that you are in my corner. Thank you, Mom and Pop, for always being here for me. Thank you, Dad for giving me a great imagination. All my kids, Kit and LaRay, Kyle, Callie, John, Jeffery, you are amazing. All my grandchildren you help me keep being. All my friends who are precious to me and like family.

Craig & Kathi and Rob & Peggy, you make everything in this so much more possible. You have always been my best friends.

Thank you, Tina Schneider and Brenda Goode Britton, for being such a wonderful PAs.

Garrett you really are the best co-author ever! I love you all. Thank you for your support! Yours, Miki Ward

Garrett - Thank you fans and supporters. Miki said it perfectly above. I could repeat it here. But who'd want to read it again? I will say, thanks for giving us the opportunity to play around with your feelings for a bit.

To my beautiful wife Kathi, without you I am not a person. To my children, thanks for the pure joy, and terror, you continually provide. Because of you, I push myself to a higher standard and sometimes, near the edge of a cliff... To my adopted children, Ethan and Kasia, thank you for making my family, your family. I love you all beyond measure

To my much older sister and my really little brother, thanks for not allowing me to follow through with my nefarious plans which I'd concocted in my youth. Still, had you allowed me, we'd all have huge houses and buffalo in our backyards!

To my Sangre de Cristo High School friends, I can't believe it's been this long. I also can't believe how amazing you are. Thank you for the fathomless love and support you've freely given me over the last four decades. – Garrett V. Ward

# OTHER BOOKS BY MIKI AND GARRETT WARD

**The Ceorfan Gargoyles Series**

Carved

Etched

Coming in the Series

Hewn

**Ceorfan Novellas**

My Tormented Mage

**Shivers Series**

We See You

Coming Sept 2019

Double Mirror

**Elser Books are Stand Alone**

Flesh and Bold

**Stand Alone by Miki Ward**

The Phantom Queen

# FIND US LINKS

FB Pages
Miki & Mine, Guys and Goyles Group
https://bit.ly/2CpH3BM

Miki's FB Author page
https://bit.ly/2yMlVSG

Garrett's FB Author page
https://bit.ly/2P3USwv

Instagram
https://bit.ly/2R05utp

Bookbub
https://bit.ly/2J3FRFh

Amazon Author Page - Follow Miki
https://amzn.to/2Ey3qrk

Amazon Author Page - Follow Garrett
https://amzn.to/2yNYOr7

www.ingramcontent.com/pod-product-compliance
Lightning Source LLC
Chambersburg PA
CBHW070504130626
46555CB00003B/1152